The Bacchanal
AND OTHER HORRIFIC TALES

DONALD MCCARTHY

TS HALL

LORRAINE NELSON

KATHRYN HEARST

SHANNON HOLLINGER

JOHN KANIECKI

RAY DEAN

JOHN ROBINSON

THOMAS KLEATON

JOE DICICCO

SEAN TAYLOR

TEEL JAMES GLENN

DREAMING BIG PUBLICATIONS

www.dreamingbigpublications.com

Contents

THE BACCHANAL ON THE ROOF

DONALD MCCARTHY

I hate waiting for my therapist to come out of her office when I have a story to tell her. The longer I sit and wait, the more I question whether I want to bring the story up, whether I want to take the chance this'll send me spiraling into another depression.

I didn't have to wait long on the night I told her about the suicide. I sat for maybe three minutes, perhaps less, before her office door opened and the previous patient, a young man with an ugly, scraggly beard, walked out. He flashed me a smile and I half suspected he was reassuring me.

In the doorway stood my therapist, Marissa, a tall woman with brown skin and large, blue eyes. I couldn't imagine she'd hit thirty-five and she might've been even younger than me. She never put on makeup, a quirk of hers I liked, as if she had nothing to hide. She wore a red plaid skirt that ended just below her knees and a purple blouse. Around her neck hung a black scarf, the type you wear inside, the type I could never pull off.

"Hello, Danielle," Marissa said. She held out her arm, welcoming me into her office. It was a nice office, designed with a minimalist taste. A leather couch snuggled up against the far wall and a wicker rocking chair sat in front of the wall to the right, a window behind it giving a street view. Across from the chair was a marble desk with one of those old computers with the huge monitor; a vase of red roses was next to it. Otherwise, the desk was spotless, which made sense since I'm pretty sure

Marissa has some OCD tendencies.

Above the desk hung Marissa's diploma. I once asked her if it was there to reassure the clients. She said sometimes the clients and sometimes herself.

I sat down on the right side of the couch, my usual spot. Marissa sat down in the rocking chair, placed her hands on her lap and smiled at me. She never talked first.

"So how are you?" I asked.

"I'm fine," she said. "I missed you last week."

I shifted, trying to find a comfortable position, but failed. My back had been tight, like someone gripping my spine, for the past week and a half. "I needed the week off because I had to collect my thoughts. There was a scene at the company party."

"Last time you told me you were dreading it. I believe you said something about it probably being like the ninth circle of hell."

"It was," I said. "It was hell right from the get go, just like I said it'd be, but the key part is the end, I guess." I paused before admitting, "I saw a woman kill herself."

"That's terrible," said Marissa, jerking back.

"I know," I said. "But it's more than just that. There's all that led to it and the nothing that followed."

Every year Tyrius Incorporated holds its "End of Summer" party at the Hotel Cabria. They don't fool around and simply rent the roof and some suites; they rent the entire hotel. Most of it doesn't get used, of course, but I'm told the element of exclusivity adds to the flavor of the party.

I took the subway to the hotel and once I reached street level I could hear dance music, the type that matches your heartbeat, the type you can feel in your chest, like it's trying to get underneath you, trying to make you not a person but part of the party.

I was fully Xanaxed which meant my mind didn't jump

around while I experienced heart palpitations- my usual state of existence in large social settings. Still, I'd begun to sweat a little on the ride over and I'd already designed excuses that'd allow me to exit conversations with at least some grace; nothing too wild, just the usual noise about having a doctor's appointment in the morning or a friend coming to town.

The bouncer outside the hotel, although he's probably referred to as something fancier, like a maître d'bouncer, smiled thinly, like his mouth was drawn with a sharp pencil point. He was muscular, but more than anything, he was greasy; I worried that if I touched his hand I'd feel a thick layer of mucus.

He asked my name, but his thin mouth never seemed to move. I mumbled "Danielle" in return and he pinned a small red rose to my blouse, his fingers pressing into me harder than I cared for.

"Right to one of the elevators," he said.

No one joined me in the elevator; a glance at my watch told me I was twenty minutes late, and there was no elevator music. Just silence. The dance music from the roof was cut off when the doors closed. The gears of the elevator made no sounds. I only knew I was ascending thanks to the red numbers above the doors: 21, 22, 23, 24, 25, 26 - the roof.

The doors moved back as quietly as curtains and the music of the party moved in, a steady beat, one that my breathing adapted to, followed by a gargle of voices, all coming together as a low, constant buzzing. A comforting breeze, still filled with summer's warmth, caressed my face as I walked out onto the roof, giving me some hope I'd survive the night.

No one looked at me as I headed to the bar. There must've been three hundred, three-fifty people up there, all of them dressed in that business casual look that says, "Hey, I'm relaxed and cool but I'm still important so go fuck off."

"How were you dressed?" Marissa asked.

"Like they were," I said.

She laughed.

"Yeah," I said. "My judgmental attitude ends up making me a hypocrite. I know. We've talked about this before."

She waved the comment away. "I'm sorry, I shouldn't have stopped you."

"Do you think I'm a hypocrite at heart?" I asked.

"No. I think you're human, like everyone else. We're one same person in the end, each of us an aspect of a larger personality."

I didn't know what she meant, but she clearly thought it was self-explanatory so I went back to my story.

They'd set up a bar in the upper right corner of the roof and I nursed a drink, vodka and cranberry juice with two ice cubes. The music didn't dominate near the bar as much so I planned to settle in for a while and observe the festivities. I knew I'd have to find my boss, Peter, and a coworker or two so it'd be clear I'd shown up. With luck they'd come over to the bar and I wouldn't have to meander out into the mob of increasingly drunk people who were letting off way too much frustration with unsubtle innuendo, giggling, and groping; groping that grew more aggressive by the minute. I didn't see one pair of eyes give off anything more than the barest sense of coherence. The crowd reminded me of ants, all crawling around, right on top of each other, with almost no awareness to how ridiculous they looked. Would they wake up the next morning and think back to this, wondering why they were so drunk, why they put their rational side away? Or would they consider it to be a necessary emotional outlet thanks to the almost sociopathic level of restraint work required of them during the week?

All the way to my left, right at the end of the bar, a man sat with his hand on the bar and his fingers spread. He twirled a pocket knife in his other hand and began to slowly stab between his fingers, picking up pace with each stab. A smug smile grew on his face but no one paid him any mind. Eventually, he stabbed himself and gave a quick cry. He stuck the finger in his drink, grimacing from the sting of the alcohol.

About five stools to the right of me, two guys, young twenties, with the same short on the sides but long on the top haircut, nodded at every woman who passed by before declaring if they'd fuck her. Their identical appearance made it seem like they were out of a very misogynistic Dr. Seuss book.

"Would not fuck," asshole one said when a slightly overweight woman walked by, struggling in her heels.

"Really?" said asshole two. "She's cute enough. Probably desperate for it. She'll let you do anything."

"Nah, that's a myth, man."

Asshole two inclined his head in my direction, apparently thinking himself slick enough that I wouldn't pick up on it.

"Maybe," whispered asshole one, putting his drink to his lips. "Love the blonde hair. Very skinny, though. Like eating disorder skinny. No ass. No boobs. Bitchy resting face."

"I'd throw her a bone," said asshole two.

Lucky me.

A soft voice behind me said, "Excuse me?"

I turned and saw an older man I vaguely recognized as one of the specters that haunted the halls of Tyrius Incorporated. He had a light grey beard and a full head of white hair that looked natural instead of the hair plugs you see on the insecure executives. His skin was wrinkled, but his bright blue eyes made up for that, giving a sense that not all humanity had been crushed out of him by his working years.

"May I buy you a drink?" he asked.

"It's an open bar," I said.

He sat down next to me. "Only reason I offered," he said. "I'm Samuel."

"I'm Danielle. I'm in accounting."

"Sorry to hear it. I'm a marketing consultant. Used to head the marketing department until a few years ago when I decided to take a step back. I'll be retiring for real come January so this is my last party."

"Congratulations," I said. "I'm sure you'll enjoy your retirement after all the stress."

"Heart attack in five years, I guarantee it," Samuel said. "But I knew that getting in. We all do, but we just push the thought."

I didn't know how to reply to that so I said nothing. Always the right course of action when you're out of your depth, but that's a lesson few have learned.

"Sorry to bring down the mood," said Samuel. A glass of bourbon had appeared in his hand, yet I'd never heard him order it. "I'm not much of a party person. After sixty years that's one thing I can say about myself with certainty."

"I'm not a party lover either," I said.

"I noticed. The pursed lips and grip of death on your drink gave it away. It's a refreshing sight compared to the rest of the crowd. I take it you're not a socializer?"

I considered the question before answering. "I don't know. Sometimes I think I am. Sometimes I think I'm not. The larger the group the more I fall in the second category."

He sipped his bourbon. "Parties always remind me of that Poe story, the one with the Red Death showing up, standing right before them yet not a one of them notices. If you haven't read it please don't disillusion me by saying so. Parties are about endings. You ever been to a New Year's party? Most depressing thing you can experience. Everyone says how the last year sucked and the next one will be great, full of surprise and success, sex and money. You go to the same party the next year and they say the exact same thing. It's madness." He set his drink down hard enough that I expected it to break.

I adjusted my red flower, not knowing how to engage with him.

"So why do you hate parties?" he asked.

"I just think it'd be real easy to attack or sexually harass someone without anyone noticing," I said. I think the drink might've been getting to me. "Scares me a bit."

"I see," Samuel said. "I better get to making the rounds. It's considered poor form if I don't make idle chit-chat with at least some of my peers."

"See you later," I said.

"Probably not," he said.

He was right. He died of a heart attack the following Thursday. There was an office email about it. I think someone brought in a condolence card to sign for his ex-wife.

"Did his death bother you?" Marissa asked.

I stared at her. "No, it made me feel amazing. How do you think I felt?"

She laughed; she always did when I was obnoxious to her, as if the whole experience was one dark joke. "You'd be surprised how many people just don't register a death unless it's someone extremely close to them. They block it out."

"If there's one thing people are good at, it's blocking things out."

I thought she'd laugh at that one, but she didn't. "Did you sign the card that went around?"

"No. I didn't see the point."

She replied with silence.

I continued my story.

It'd reached eleven o'clock when I decided to venture away from the bar. I'd had three drinks and felt some degree of bravery. My gait was slightly askew, my feet at too much of an angle, probably because of the mix of Xanax and alcohol. The prescription bottle said not to consume both within a twelve hour period, but parties are made for bad decision-making so I actually managed to fit in on that count.

The music grew louder the further into the crowd I ventured. I couldn't quite pinpoint its source or I'd have tried to keep a safe distance. Some old Shakira song was blasting and I vaguely remembered seeing a music video for it back in high school and thinking, *Fuck, that's who I gotta compete with for the boys' attention?*

The people around me, and it was hard to believe they were the same faceless, lifeless coworkers I passed on a daily basis, looked determined to enjoy themselves, throwing themselves into the party, trying their best to move with the music, to fit in, to be a part of the experience. A few people approached me and shouted over the music; I think I knew them. I shouted back at them, but I don't remember what I said. I'm sure it was generic.

The Shakira song morphed into a dance house version of "Tainted Love," a version which omitted the BWAMP BWAMP part of the song that you have no choice but to clap along with. How anyone could think removing that was a good idea was beyond me.

I spotted Peter dancing with a woman from marketing, I'm pretty sure her name was Jennifer, and he winked at me. I winked back. I counted this as an interaction and did a mental pat on the back.

Dancing bodies went by me quickly and one very intoxicated man attempted to dance with me. His breath reeked and his full, red face told me he was a barely functioning alcoholic on the best of days. He smiled at me as he attempted to dance, waiting for me to join him. I just stared until he went away.

A woman with bulging, bloodshot eyes came by, stopping in front of me only for a second, long enough to turn and scream in my face, her scream teetering on the edge of insanity, full of joy and hate. I took a few steps back and she evaporated into the crowd. My cocktail of alcohol and medication prevented me from suffering a panic attack.

"Summertime Sadness" began to play, a song I didn't mind. The dancers didn't adjust themselves to the song's slower beat. Standing still, probably looking like an awkward prom date, I briefly wondered what it'd be like to dance to the song. To move slowly, elegantly, across the roof, to have some element of grace, to have the music complement me instead of overwhelm me. Did such a version of me exist? Was that me hidden in my head, repressed? Or had I murdered that version of me long ago? This was not the first moment in my life when grief for the wasted past meets a weird streak of optimism for the future.

I came back to the reality of the party (such moments of introspection rarely last) and my bearings returned. I squirmed through the crowd and arrived back at the bar. I spotted a couple near the elevator, kissing, practically eating each other's faces. The man smashed his groin against the woman, trying to fuck her with his clothes on. The woman's hands were on his neck. At first I thought she was holding him as they kissed, but no, nothing so mundane. She was choking him, gently, releasing every few seconds before resuming.

The man with the knife was back to stabbing between his fingers, this time watched by a crowd of four, all of whom appeared dissatisfied until he once again missed the mark and stabbed himself. He shoved his finger back into his drink and one of the onlookers said, "Two hundred bucks if you drink that."

The man shrugged, removed his finger, and downed his bloody cocktail. The onlookers applauded.

A drunk woman ran by, I recognized her as someone from HR, heading for the elevator, vomiting just before she reached it. Chunks of vomit slid down her dress, hitting her feet. She wiped at her face with her hands, flinging the vomit to the floor.

I decided to have one more drink before leaving this place.

"I'm sorry to interrupt you," said Marissa, "but our time is almost up."

My pulse quickened in anger, but I did my best not to show it. Couldn't she see I was getting somewhere? "Okay."

9

"I just wanted to make sure we at least touched on what you wanted to talk about."

"I wanted to talk about all of this," I said. "The suicide was just the whole party narrowed down to five brutal seconds. It was the way the party wanted the night to end. Perhaps it was how we all knew it would end."

Asshole one and asshole two were still at the bar when I ordered my fourth, at least I think it was my fourth, drink. I didn't hear them declaring who they'd fuck and who they wouldn't; maybe they'd run out of women. The party's music had returned to the techno beat it had been projecting when I first arrived and the heartbeat of the party returned in full force, infecting even my drink, the liquid pulsating with each beat. I downed it fast, my face flushing, my head not ready for another infusion of alcohol.

Even far from the heart of the party I could sense the desperation, the excitement, the unleashed rush of emotions, as if the feelings themselves danced around me, daring me to embrace them, to let loose, to be in a state of release.

I didn't know it at the time, but by this point the woman was already on the ledge.

Asshole two said, "What the hell is going on over there?" His voice had such sharp urgency that I turned, mildly intrigued.

I saw her on the ledge. She wore a black dress which contrasted with her blonde hair. She couldn't have been older than thirty, maybe not even twenty-five. She spread her arms, as if presenting herself to us, asking if we approved. The party halted to look at her, every person glancing over, making certain the scene would be worth their time. The music didn't stop, but it faded, as if muffled by the party's interest in a new scene.

The woman swayed, her dress allowing her to blend in with the night, as if only her head, extremities, and red rose existed, her body absorbed by the night. She reached for her red rose and ripped it from her dress, a long strand of black string flying out with it, disappearing into the dark. Her eyes blinked faster than should be possible. She was both here and elsewhere.

She let go of the rose and took a step backwards. She stood there, one foot on the ledge and one foot in the air. It probably wasn't long, but I remember that second the most, the second where she hung there, when the possibility remained she might not descend.

She did, of course. It was fast. I can't even recall seeing her fall and I don't think she screamed.

She stood in front of us and then she didn't.

"At the risk of sounding cliché," said Marissa, "how does all of this make you feel?"

I held out my right arm, my palm open. "Like I'm letting something loose."

"Pain?"

"No, not pain. Not guilt. Blindness maybe."

"How so?"

I struggled to find the right words. "I… I mean, it wasn't exactly like how I described it. It's how I remember it, yeah, but I don't know if it's how it actually happened. You see, the following Monday there was a donation box for some sort of suicide fund. There was a picture of her next to it, too. Her hair was black in the picture. I asked someone from her department and they said it'd always been black. Never blond."

Marissa said nothing and neither did I. I looked at the clock and noticed we were a minute from the end of the session.

Marissa broke our shared silence by saying, "Your story is as true as it needs to be for our purposes. If it's in our mind then there's at least some truth to it. We like to think of ourselves as beings made of spirit and thought, but our minds are just electrical impulses, shooting out images. If your mind is thinking it then it's real in some sense. It exists. It's been made. What do you think this thought's existence means?"

"I don't know. What do you think it means?"

"That's not for me to say. Annoying, I know."

I sat in silence again and I appreciated Marissa giving me the time to do so. "I know this is so horribly narcissistic considering this woman died and I'm here and fine, yet I can't shake the feeling that if the party hadn't snared her and put her up there then it would've been me. The party would've grabbed me, maybe when I had my moment of introspection in the crowd, and guided me to my end. Maybe if I'd arrived ten minutes earlier I would've been the victim."

"You realize there's no higher intelligence that is the party. It's just people."

I snorted, an unpleasant tic of mine. "Yes, I know that. It didn't feel like that at the time, though. It felt like every pent up feeling, every anxiety, every horror that we all usually hid, somehow existed at once, in the DNA of that night, and it grew to such a level it had to be expelled or all hell would break loose on that rooftop. And the woman did it for us. She ended the ritual. We all went home after her death. No one talked much about it. It's like it didn't quite happen, like you've always been home and you can wash away the memories of the strange place. Her death allowed us to leave, to abandon the wild party, to view it all as a brief flash of twisted reality. But for some reason I can't abandon that night. I can't just go home and let the memory fade. I feel like I need to still see it."

"Speaking of going home, we need to end." Marissa stood up and I followed her example. "I know it's unpleasant to have to end like this."

Considering it took me a moment to find my balance once I was on my feet, I agreed.

"Yeah, it's weird."

"We'll talk more about this in the future, I'm sure."

She opened the door and I had to walk out. A patient sat in the waiting room, a young woman, early twenties at the latest, and she immediately looked away, embarrassed to be seen. Her hair was dyed purple, her skin blemished, and she was familiar in a way I couldn't put my finger on.

I smiled at her, hoping she caught it out of the corner of her eye.

THE END

About the Author: Donald McCarthy is a writer and a teacher. He has published in anthologies and magazines, his work ranging from horror to articles on the economy. He is afraid of cheese. His website is www.donaldmccarthy.com

The Encouragement Specialists

TS Hall

It was nothing like Darren Jenkins expected, and he scrambled for the business card in the pocket of his jeans to make sure the address was correct.

STARTUP TALENT

Talent Assurance Agents

19 Riverfront Terrace

We'll Make Your Dreams Come True

"It's just an old warehouse," Darren said to the empty night air. He stood in the parking lot, alone in the Riverfront district, despite his better judgment, and the agent his Professor had assured him would be, "Worth the trip" were in a damn, dirty old warehouse.

"This does not instill confidence," he said, again to himself.

The wind blew, colder than usual for an evening in late May, and he shivered. He'd tell Professor Wilkes he had cruised by and found the place lacking in the necessary décor for a late night stop. Hell, even most criminals knew better than to walk the Riverfront at night.

Just then the door to the warehouse banged open and a youngish woman, in her early thirties and mildly attractive in the dopey housewife kind of way, dropped a box of books with a loud, "Dammit!" Darren, a lifetime of gentlemanly upper class upbringing (and a keen eye for noticing a quick chance to make a good impression with the opposite sex) jogged the last few yards to the warehouse, casually flicking his hand behind him and pressing the key to lock up the BMW.

"Hold on, I'll help," he said, flashing his most non-threatening smile. If he was afraid to be here this late, he could only imagine how scared she must be. She dropped to one knee, cradling the cardboard box to her body, and plucked the books up with a hand, flinging them into the box in frustration.

"Thanks, I'm a bit of a klutz," she said. She looked up at him, a smile with pretty, white teeth and good skin for a woman her age, and he thought he might ask her for a drink later after all. She was pretty enough, for one night at least.

"It's nothing I haven't done a thousand times," Darren said, dropping the last book, a beat-up Patterson novel, back into the box. He stood with her, smacking his hands on his jeans, and offered her his hand. "Darren Jenkins," he said.

"Oh, uh," she scooted her right arm around the box to show him that it ended at the wrist. She squeezed the box against her middle, framing her breasts, and abruptly squeezed with her left hand. "Sally Harold."

"A pleasure," he said, fight to keep from staring at her stump. His smile faltered a bit, but he recovered, knowing the drink wouldn't be happening after all.

"Are you here for an appointment?" Sally asked, her eyebrows going up at the end of the sentence.

"Yeah, my Professor set something up with… this place," he fetched the card out of his pocket once more. "Startup Talent Agency?"

"Congratulations," she said. She did a light curtsey and almost dropped the box. This time, he didn't offer to help. She looked him up and down. "You an actor?"

"Writer actually."

"Oh really. Fiction, poetry, plays?"

"Literary Fiction."

She wrinkled her nose and he laughed. "Sorry," she said, "Haven't had many good experiences with fiction writers. They're all too good at lying."

15

"Maybe you haven't met the right ones," Darren said, mentally kicking himself. He looked at the stump once more to remind himself that he didn't need to waste his charm.

"Maybe not." She looked back through the door and leaned in close. Her face grew cold and direct. "Word of advice?"

"Sure."

"Do what you have to do. Just listen to Mr. Nunziata, he'll get you through. You may not think so at times, but it's worth it in the end."

She seemed hesitant and scurried away like a field mouse. "Hey," he called, before she could get across the parking lot. "You a client?" A sharp nod. "Can they fulfill their promise?" Three nods, emphatic, and she was around a van and out of sight.

He watched her shuffle away and turned back to study the warehouse. It was clean; cleaner than any of the surrounding buildings. And, the parking lot was well kept, no stray cigarette butts, no fast food wrappers in sight. "What the hell," he said and stepped inside.

The inside was exactly what Darren had originally expected. Rows of cubicles, empty at this time of night, ran along the walls with a large waiting area, complete with leather couches and a clean, bland business carpet. A single desk sat by the door; a disinterested woman sat tapping away at a computer.

"May I help you?" she asked, raising her head. She was beautiful, no more than twenty, her hair as black as ink poured to the tips of her shoulders, her lips a deep red beneath clear blue eyes. Darren felt the smile return, and shoved one hand in his pocket as he approached the desk. The placard said MISS MELONY.

"I'm here to see Mr. Nunziata, appointment set up by Professor Wilkes." She nodded and pounded his name into the keyboard with long thick nails as red as her lips. When she turned away, Darren tilted his eyes down her low cut blouse to make sure she had come by her name honestly.

"You the writer?" she asked.

"Yeah, Darren Jenkins," he said, offering her his hand. She stood and shook, her hand darting into his and away like a serpent.

"You're late."

He pulled his phone from his pocket to check the time. "Only five minutes though, right?" He gave her a small wink and it passed by, ignored. He exhaled loudly through his nose and tried to smile. He must have left his charm outside with the mousy housewife.

"Mr. Nunziata suggested I show you to his office the moment you arrived. If you arrived," she corrected. She held out her hand, pointing to the left side of the office.

"Lead on."

He followed past the rows of cubicles, glancing at the names on the doors while sneaking peeks at the way her skirt danced. At the end of the aisle, a set of stairs led up to a mahogany office door with a shining brass handle. Miss Melony stopped at the bottom and stepped aside. "Mr. Nunziata's office. I messaged him to let him know you were coming."

"Thanks," Darren said, and decided her ass was fine enough for one more attempt, "Hey, could you keep an eye on my car? It's the BMW by the door."

"Sure, I'll stop doing my job to watch your car," she said dismissively and strolled back to her desk.

Bitch.

He climbed the stairs and stood at the door, drawing his hand back to knock when a voice from the inside shouted, "Come on in, Mr. Jenkins."

The office was as efficient as the waiting room. Clean, standard business class, nothing exotic. An organized desk sat in the middle of the room and a man stood at it with his hands behind his back, staring at Darren. He extended a hand and pointed to the leather chair, crossing the room to take the opposite seat. Darren sat. The man took the seat across from him and crossed his legs with keen precision. He continued to stare at Darren, a wry smile, unspeaking. The light reflected off the slight grey at his temples, making him seem almost regal.

"Mr. Nunziata?" Darren asked, when the silence had grown uncomfortable. The hairs on his neck stood up and he rolled his shoulders to dislodge the sensation of being watched.

"That is correct. I assume you are Darren Jenkins, the student Wally Wilkes has told me about?"

"That is correct," Darren replied mimicking the brisk manor and inflection Mr. Nunziata had used.

"And did he tell you what we do here?" Mr. Nunziata asked. His hands appeared atop his knees, interlocked and perfectly manicured.

"He told me you guys were the reason he was finally published. That you helped him write and sell his first three novels."

"I believe he prefers to say, 'They lit a fire under my ass and made me get the bullshit out of my ears' right?" he said, his voice turning into a damn good representation of Professor Wilkes.

Darren laughed, the chill in the room slipping away like a foul odor, "I believe that's exactly the way he put it."

Mr. Nunziata laughed once, a quick bark really, and rolled his eyes. "That's Wally, as predictable as the sunset. He seems to think you have a fair bit of talent, Mr. Jenkins."

"Darren, please," he said, leaning over to offer his hand. His father has always insisted that he meet everyone with a firm handshake. It told them you weren't afraid of being touched and that you weren't a pussy, two facts that had served him well in New York law offices.

"Darren. You can call me Todd." They shook.

"I've been reading over a sample your Professor sent me, Darren. It's good. You show talent, more than most of the clients we have already signed."

"Gee, Todd, you're gonna make me blush," Darren said. He didn't do false modesty.

"We like to think of ourselves as more than agents here,

Mr. Jenkins. We are facilitators of our clients. We set up parameters, we encourage our clients when they falter, and we see to it that they meet their end goal. As such, we offer a 100% guarantee to every person we sign. You will succeed if you sign with us-"

"Or?" Darren said, interrupting Todd. Todd breathed in and his face grew red, but the smile never left his lips.

"We do not think in the negatives, and we have never had cause to. We have worked with thirty writers over the years and every one of them has found publication. Sixty percent even made the best seller's list, like your Professor and his first book."

Darren wanted to snort and call bullshit - no one had a perfect track record - but watching Todd's face, he thought better of interrupting. He'd let the man go through his spiel. His confidence was entertaining.

"You will be assigned an Encouragement Specialist, someone to keep tabs on you and make sure you are meeting your end of the bargain. We typically start out at five thousand words a week and contract our clients for their first two novels. Do you think that would be doable?"

Darren could write five thousand words in a good day, when the words were flowing and he had his muse by the throat. "I think I could manage," Darren said. "What's your percentage?" Always get to the money, as soon as possible. He'd heard of agents that held their writer's hands before, and though he didn't think he really needed a babysitter, it would come down to the numbers.

"Twelve percent. Lower than most of your standard commissions for first time authors."

Darren whistled. That was a damn good rate. "What's the catch?"

"No catch. I run this company at break even, Darren. I'm not here for your money. I just want your talent." A smile spread across his face, ear to ear. A do-gooder, then, Darren decided.

"Well, this sounds like an amazing offer, but I'll have to think it over."

"Obviously. We never let our clients sign on the first day. How about we agree to meet again tomorrow night, same time. I'm a night owl and get my best work done after the sun goes down."

"Sure, sounds good."

"Excellent." He stood and offered his hand to Darren, clapping him on the back. "I want you to really consider this, Mr. Jenkins. We promise you success. I personally guarantee that if you sign with us you will get a book published, with a reputable publisher, none of that self-publishing bullshit. But, we are organized here, a company of sticklers. Once you sign with us, we expect you to hold up to your end of the bargain." Darren stepped past Mr. Nunziata and rolled his eyes. He hated lectures.

Miss Melony greeted him as he walked through the door, with a perfect smile on her face and hand on his arm, the indifferent attitude from the previous encounter replaced with chipper flirtatiousness. "Good evening, Mr. Jenkins. How are you today?" she asked, with a quick wink and bob of the head, hard enough to make her chest jiggle alluringly.

"Better now," Darren said. He glanced down her low cut blouse again, his pants stirring at the sight of a lace black bra barely visible. He raised his eyes to hers and realized he'd been caught. She winked his concern away and led him to the back.

"Mr. Nunziata is expecting you, of course," she said as they walked. She leaned in closer and whispered in his ear, "He says you're the next big thing, that you show a lot of promise." The feel of her breath on his ear made his heart rise into his throat. He could grow to like seeing Miss Melony.

She stopped at the stairs once more, returning his arm. "I hope we'll be seeing you more often, Mr. Jenkins."

"I hope I'll be seeing more of you, Miss Melony," he

winked back and sprang up the steps. Mr. Nunziata was waiting at the top of the stairs, the door open. He beckoned Darren into the room and shut the door behind him. Darren took the same seat without invitation and plucked the contract from the glass tabletop. An expensive pen sat next to it, the cap off and waiting.

"Right to business it seems," Mr. Nunziata said with another barking laugh.

"My father's a judge…"

"Judge Jenkins, Eighth district; we've done our homework, on your family as well as your capabilities," Mr. Nunziata said.

Daren paused for a minute, puzzling the statement over before he returned to reading. "Right, he's a judge and he made sure to instill in his son the divine commandment, 'Thou Shalt Read The Fine Print Before Thou Signest.'"

"By all means," Mr. Nunziata said, taking the opposite seat to watch him read.

"Looks like the first page is a standard NDA?"

"Correct, Mr. Jenkins." They were back to formalized names, strictly business now. "We have to ensure that our practices, primarily pertaining to our Encouragement Program, are confidential. There's a reason we're the only agency that issues a 100% guarantee."

That made sense. Darren shuffled through to the next document and read. It was mostly standard legalese regarding the percentage, the guarantee, nothing untoward. "It says you want the five thousand words by midnight every Friday night?"

"That's right. Your Encouragement Specialist will designate a meeting location. You will hand deliver five thousand words worth of…" he paused and his face clouded, "are you one of the throwback types that writes everything on a legal pad?"

"No, strictly computers for me."

"Good. You will give him printed pages totaling at least five thousand words. The clock will reset. Anything in excess of five thousand words does not roll over to the next week.

Simple, right?"

"Sure." He scanned the documents. Nothing jumped out at him. Everything looked to be part of the standard writing contract. He picked up the pen and scrawled his name on the last page, making sure to initial the highlighted areas, and then pushed the forms across the table. His first agent. A brief sense of pride flooded his chest.

The first week passed like a first kiss. The words flowed and he passed the requirement by Tuesday, but he kept at it, the driving force of a deadline pushing him forward. On Thursday he got a call from his Encouragement Specialist.

"Mr. Jenkins?"

"Yeah, this is Darren."

"I am your Encouragement Specialist. My name is Nedry." His voice was low and deep, a thunderstorm on the plains. He spoke very curtly, as if he had rehearsed. "Would you prefer to bring the pages to me, or have me come to you?"

"It would be great if you could come to me." Any chance to stay out of the Riverfront.

"Thank you. Sit the pages by your apartment door by midnight. I will collect them." He hung up.

That didn't exactly sound encouraging.

Darren waited until ten o'clock on Friday evening. With the spring semester over, most of his classmates had scooted back home to bumfuck Idaho, and he had never made any friends in town. He printed the pages, choosing to go with everything he'd pumped out that week instead of stopping at the required five thousand words, and dropped them by the door in a neat little pile. "This hardly seems professional," he said before getting back inside.

An hour later he checked and the pages were gone.

His phone buzzed, waking him from a deep sleep. "The

fuck," Darren muttered, slapping at the nightstand for the phone. The time read almost noon. "Hello?"

"Mr. Jenkins, did I wake you?"

"Yeah, late night. Pounding that muse into submission." He'd watch an entire season of anime before going to bed. One he'd already seen twice.

"Let me offer my apologies. Your first week went very well. I have the pages in front of me and they are to my satisfaction." Darren furrowed his brow and rubbed at his eyes. He didn't realize his work would be judged like a cut of beef.

"Thanks."

"At startup, Mr. Jenkins, we are firm believers in the carrot and the stick. Are you familiar with the idiom?"

"Yeah, eats or beats."

Mr. Nunziata laughed. "Yes, indeed! Eats or beats; I think I will steal that."

"Feel free; it's not one of mine."

"Given your excellent output in your first week, and given that we want to instill confidence in our relationship, Mr. Jenkins, I have spoken to Mr. Nedry and we have elected to give you your first taste of the carrot this week. We won't promise you a prize at the conclusion of every week, but we will issue similar rewards from time to time." There was a knock at the door to his apartment. "Enjoy, Mr. Jenkins."

He jumped out of bed in his boxers and yawned as he walked across the floor of his studio apartment, kicking at a few absentminded piles of clothes along the way. "I hope this isn't a normal occurrence; I'm not much of a morning person," he said as he opened the door.

Miss Melony stood in the doorway in a long coat. "Something tells me you won't mind," she said, pulling the coat open. She was naked underneath, and her body was better than he'd imagined. Darren's mouth fell open. She put a hand on his chest and pushed him back into the apartment, towards the empty bed.

Even with the incentive of Miss Melony, Darren had a good month. The pages were always on time, and Nedry always pulled the vanishing trick within an hour of their arrival by his door. It wasn't until the thick of summer arrived, and Darren found himself a third of the way through the novel, that trouble arrived.

He wasn't happy with the direction. He knew his opening was soft, that he'd introduced one character too many, and he felt the weight of the narrative, and the eventual destination of his plot, sliding from his grasp like a bar of soap. The harder he tried to push forward, the more entangled his story seemed to be. The phrase "Writer's Block" flashed behind his head in neon lights, a headache forming whenever he sat at the computer and struggled for more than an hour. By Wednesday, he'd written barely a thousand new words before giving up and returning to the first chapter. He reworked the opening, took out the mouthy black friend he'd woven in purely to make sure he was reaching a wider demographic, and come Friday, he dropped the pages at the door. The opening was shorter by a page, but tighter, and he felt that he could continue the story now, though he would need to spend most of the next month rewriting.

The next morning, before the sun had even cleared the horizon, he was awoken by a hard knock. He checked the clock and rolled out of the bed, hoping for a second encounter with Miss Melony. He opened the door without bothering to check.

"Here, hold this," Miss Melony said, handing him her purse. The coat was gone, but she looked equally fine in her regular blouse and skirt.

"What, why…"

She was on her knees before he could finish the thought, tugging at his boxers and wrapping her lips around him. Darren tucked the purse under his arm and leaned against the doorframe, looking out into the hall to see if anyone was up.

"Just let me know when you're close," she said.

It wasn't long before Darren dropped his hand to the back of her head, his fingers sliding in her dark curls, and moaned, "Almost." She squeezed his shaft at the base and pulled away, opening her mouth. Darren closed his eyes.

And an enormous pain enveloped him, dropping him to the floor.

He was unable to scream. A vast ache bloomed throughout his abdomen. He clutched at his groin and cracked one eye. She'd punched him in the balls, her hand decked in expensive rings. Miss Melony massaged her knuckles in the manner of someone accustomed to violence. She stood over him and wiped at her mouth, making sure her lipstick was in order. "Mr. Nunziata wants you in the office by noon."

"You bitch," Darren muttered.

She smiled and bent to pat him on the cheek. "No hard feelings, Mr. Jenkins. Get your shit together and maybe next time I'll make it up to you." She ran a hand down his chest and tweaked his nipple. The sudden arousal made his balls ache that much harder.

"What happens if I tell him to fuck off?" Darren managed to roll into a sitting position, his legs tucked beneath him, and leaned against the doorframe.

Miss Melony smiled as wide as a carnival, "Oh, honey, you don't want to do that."

"Mr. Jenkins, come in, please." His smile was slight, lips pressed tightly together. An undertaker's smile. Darren limped across the carpet to his customary chair and eased himself down, his balls still swollen. "Would you like some ice?" Nunziata asked, the smile growing into a wry smirk.

"Fuck you."

"The carrot and the stick, Mr. Jenkins. You were warned."

"I came by to tell you to tear up the contract. I'm through with this shit. I've called my father and…"

"Yes, the honorable Judge Jenkins; we anticipated that," Nunziata said. He reached into his jacket and pulled out a phone, slid it across the table. "He's on hold right now, waiting to talk to you."

"What?"

"Your father is on the phone right now, Mr. Jenkins. He wishes to have a word with you."

Darren picked up the phone, humoring him. "Who the hell is this," he said, his voice full of anger.

"Shut up, son," his father said. The voice was unmistakable. His father, a chain smoker for most of his life, spoke like two slabs of granite fucking in an alleyway. "I got your message. Do what Mister Nunziata says and write the damn book."

"What the fuck, Dad; how can…"

"Shut up, Darren. You don't know the type of people you're dealing with. Remember the Hawkins trial?" His father had presided over the Hawkins trial, a case of a mob informant swinging against one of the major mafia families. The trial ended when the mob informant was found bound in the trunk of a police car. He had choked to death with his cock stuffed in his mouth. "Do what they say." The call ended.

Mr. Nunziata slid into the seat across from him, placing his hands on his knees in calculated arrogance. "Why are you doing this?" Darren asked. "I gave you five thousand words."

"You gave us a rewrite. That will not work."

"Why the fuck not? I'm the writer; I know where the story's going. If I didn't go back…"

"Correction, Mr. Jenkins. You want to be a writer. That's why you came to us."

"Whatever, I'm the one…"

"No!" Mr. Nunziata darted forward and slapped both hands on the table, sending the pens and papers flying into the floor. Darren jerked away, pain blossoming in his testicles from the sudden movement. "You don't get to dismiss it that easy. You wanted us to make sure you wrote a novel. That's what we are going to do." He leaned back in the chair and pushed a stray hair back into place. "No rewrites. New content every week."

"I never agreed to that, I…"

"You agreed to whatever we say, Mr. Jenkins."

Darren scrubbed at his face. "Why are you doing this? Why can't I write this book the way I want to?"

"The way you do things doesn't work, Mr. Jenkins, or you never would have come to us. Why are we doing this?" He lifted his fingers, pointing towards the ceiling. "Maybe I'm a good Catholic boy and see your wasted potential as a mortal sin?" He stood up and looked out the window by his door, down into the offices. "My uncle started this business. Back then, he specialized in quitting. Smoking, cheating, playing the ponies, it didn't matter. If you wanted to stop doing something and were too weak to quit, he could see to it that it happened."

He turned back to Darren. The smile returned and with it, the fervor of a Pentecostal preacher burning in his eyes. "But, what good is quitting, Darren? Anyone can make you stop doing something. You just take it away from them." Darren swallowed, believing himself in the room with a madman.

"Where's the challenge? Where's the sense of accomplishment? Don't they say, 'you can lead a horse to water, but you can't make him drink'? You want him to stop drinking, you take away the water; but to make him drink, there's the rub, so to speak. Our company is about making you drink, Mr. Jenkins. And, once we have, we've made a contribution to the world. If we can twist your arms and make you put out even one book, then we've succeeded. We've added something to the world." He winked, "And, maybe saved your soul to boot."

He was crazy, fanatical, Darren was sure of it. "What happens if I don't? What happens if I refuse to give you any more pages?"

"The next time we don't have five thousand word on your door by your scheduled time, you get to meet Mr. Nedry face to face. If you fail to meet your obligation after that, once you are able to write again, of course," he interjected with a hand on Darren's shoulder, "Then, Mr. Darren Jenkins, if you fail once more, we make things harder for you."

"Harder… what does that mean?"

"If neither the carrot nor the stick work out, we take drastic measures. Some people require a challenge; they need to rise to the occasion. They find their inspiration with their backs to the wall."

Darren began to shake, from pain, from fear. "What does that mean?"

"Mr. Jenkins, do you really want to find out?"

Darren made it back to his apartment and stared at his laptop like a riddle, unable to form a coherent thought. He stared at his screen, the space below the cursor waiting like an ominous maw. He put his fingers to the keys and felt them tremble. He plucked at the keys until a sentence formed.

"I can't do this," he said, slamming the lid. He paced the apartment and grabbed his coat. He'd never needed a drink so bad in his life.

At the bar, he took a seat in the corner. He had the waitress bring him a beer and looked over the minimal menu offered, the idea of food making his stomach sour. He played the conversation over in his head. He was fucked. He'd been here before, three times. Always at roughly a third of the way through his novels he hit the wall. He would find the story disappearing like a handful of smoke. He didn't know why it happened, but it always did. Only, this time it was apt to get him hurt.

"I'll go to the police," he muttered to himself. "I'll go to the cops and let them handle it." The memory of the headlines after the Hawkins trial came to mind, the images popularized by the trashy tabloids filling him with dread. His beer came and he drank it quick, then ordered another.

He spent the first half of the week drunk, wandering from the bar to his apartment, occasionally stopping by the liquor store on the corner to bring a bottle home with him. He woke up Thursday morning in a cold sweat, realizing less than two days remained and he had the full five thousand words to go. He spent the day at the keyboard typing and deleting sentences, the tension growing, and with it, his inability to write.

When he was still four thousand words short on Friday morning he began to panic, rocking back and forth in front of his computer. "Just write, just fucking write," spilling from his lips like a prayer. When nothing would come, he opened his files and began to dig for something he had already written, something that could be doctored to fit. He found a short story he'd written his freshmen year, almost entirely sensory and stream of consciousness. With a couple hundred words of editing and a quick change of the character's name he was done. He looked at the clock by his bedside and saw that he had barely an hour remaining. He dropped the pages by the door, spilling them with shaking hands.

"Get up, Mr. Jenkins," a voice said, floating out of the darkness. A light flicked on by his bedside.

Darren bolted upright in his bed. "What the hell are you doing in my apartment?" Mr. Nunziata stood by the footboard, his arms behind his back. He brought them forward and tossed the pages, the ones he'd left by the door only four hours ago, onto the bed.

"Mr. Jenkins, I'd like you to meet your Encouragement Specialist, Mr. Nedry." Beside Mr. Nunziata stood a monster, well over six and a half feet tall, layers of muscle covered by tattoos beneath a t-shirt one size too small. He held a gun, dwarfed by his mammoth hands. He nodded, his face as impassive as stone.

"I gave you your pages," Darren said, crawling back against the bed until his back was pressed against the wall above the headboard.

"No, you repurposed a story you wrote three years ago. I told you, we did our homework." He stepped aside. "Leave his hands and face alone, Mr. Nedry, the rest you may do with as you wish."

Nedry smiled, the opportunity to inflict pain breaking through the impasse of emotions. He put the gun in his pocket and approached the bed. Darren rolled away and tried to run, but he didn't get far.

Nedry caught a foot and pulled him to the floor, pinning him between his knees. He used his fists first, slamming them into Darren's back like the head of a sledgehammer. Six blows, three on each side of his spine, three to each kidney. His punches were economical, delivered with enough force to administer the maximum amount of pain. Darren curled into a ball and tried to cover as much of himself as possible. Nedry stood and drove a foot into Darren's ribs, then his stomach. Darren felt a rib snap and screamed, "I'll write it, please stop!"

"Shut him up," Mr. Nunziata told Nedry. Miss Melony laughed.

Nedry kicked him in the stomach again. His boots were steel tipped and Darren felt all of the air forced out his lungs. He gasped for air and fought to breathe. Tears streamed down his face. "That enough?" he heard Nedry ask Mr. Nunziata.

Mr. Nunziata scratched his jaw, contemplating the pain on Darren's face as he struggled for air. "Did you break anything? You could do his legs? Or, maybe just one ankle?"

"I broke one of his ribs. That's going to hurt like hell all week. I'll break his legs if you want, but that means we'll have to get a doc in here to set the break, or risk him dying."

Mr. Nunziata gave a wave of dismissal. "Yes, all right. Give him a few shots to the balls and we'll be done with it."

After, Nedry carried him into the bathroom and laid him in the tub. "Make sure the stopper is gone, we don't want him to accidently drown," Mr. Nunziata said. Nedry grunted and ripped the plug out of the drain, cracking the porcelain tub. In the back of Darren's mind, the part unclouded by pain, he realized that the damage to the tub would eat his deposit, and tried to laugh. Blood spurted out of his mouth and he coughed.

Nedry turned on the shower. "If you go to the hospital or the police, you'll be dead by the end of the day. You have the next week off, Mr. Jenkins. Use it to recover and focus."

Nunziata paused by the bathroom door, surveying the trail of blood leading from the bed to the bathroom. "It would be unwise of you to miss another deadline."

It was a week of slow agony. Miss Melony stopped by the next day to bring him food. Before she left, she pulled her top down, a quick flash of her tits. "Remember, Mr. Jenkins, you could always choose the carrot."

"Fuck you."

She swayed her hips as she strolled out the door and called, "Write your words and maybe you can."

Darren was still pissing blood, and breathing felt like nails being raked through his chest, when Friday came around. He could walk again, albeit with a limp, but sitting for longer than five minutes was hell on earth, his kidneys and spine still heavily bruised from Nedry's encouragement. His laptop sat at his desk like a wayward talisman, the solution to his problems if only he could put his fingers to the keys and write. He took Tylenol by the handful, and the image of an empty bottle lying in the sink, his body cold on the bathroom floor began to have a certain appeal.

No, he wasn't a coward. And he wouldn't let some shithead Mafioso with a backwards philosophy of religion get the best of him. He was a Jenkins, dammit!

But, the longer he sat at the computer, the more he ached, and the words hid from him. The unspoiled page taunted him like a dream he couldn't quite remember. Friday became Tuesday and an uncontrollable terror seized Darren. He wasn't going to be able to write, not under these conditions. His muse, as he imagined her, had always been a delicate thing, coaxed out of the shadows with gentle kisses and sweet words. Mr. Nunziata was trying to set fire to the forest to drive her out, and it wouldn't work.

On Wednesday, he resigned to get away. He would run.

He had over a million dollars in his trust funds, more than enough to start a new life somewhere, preferably outside the United States. He knew they would look for him, but with his money he could make it difficult. In his experience, if things were difficult long enough, most people would just give up.

He grabbed a bag, tossed in a couple changes of clothes, his toiletries, his passport. He raided his hiding places, gathering all the cash he had scattered throughout the apartment, better than a couple grand. He zipped the bag and scanned the room to see if he had forgotten anything. After a minute, he scooped up the laptop. They would scour the hard drive for his work, and he refused to let Nunziata see one more word.

He called a cab and waited, staring out the window until it hit the curb. He bounded down the stairs two at a time, jumped into the back and told the cabbie to book it for the airport. He would by a ticket there, in cash, so there would be no trail. From his next stop, he would buy another ticket, until he could get out of the States.

The cab made it a block before a siren sounded and the red and blue flashes of a patrol car filled the rearview mirror. "It's just the cops, you'll be fine," he whispered to himself, as the flat foot approached the car. Instead of going to the driver, the officer stopped by the back window and tapped on the glass with his gun.

"Out of the car, Mr. Jenkins. Mr. Nunziata needs to have a word with you."

The officer threw him in the back and drove him to the warehouse. Nedry was waiting by the door, the gun back in his hand. He grunted a thank you as the officer pushed Darren through the door. Miss Melony shook her head as Darren began to cry, shambling between the cubicles like a death row inmate.

Mr. Nunziata waited in his office, this time behind the big oak desk. The carpet was covered in plastic.

"I'm sorry! I'll write!" Darren blubbered. Nedry pushed him to his knees before the desk. "I'll write five thousand words a day! Please don't kill me!"

"Kill you, Mr. Jenkins?" Mr. Nunziata gave him a perplexed look. "We're not going to kill you. How could we make good on our guarantee if we were to kill you?"

Darren stopped crying and looked at the plastic under his knees. "But, the plastic?"

"Oh, there will be bloodshed. You've earned that," he nodded to Nedry and Darren felt a punch on the back of his head, sending him to the floor. "Trying to run? Did you think we weren't watching you? We've had a camera in your apartment since you signed the contract, Mr. Jenkins." Darren's world was spinning; his head felt like a cracked egg.

"We consider fleeing a violation of our trust, an attempt to sever the contract. I told you if you didn't hold up your end of the agreement we would make things harder on you, didn't I, Mr. Jenkins?" He was picked up and slammed to the ground again, the air flying from his lungs. Nedry knelt and pressed a knee the size of a melon into the center of Darren's back and stretched Darren's arms wide.

Mr. Nunziata opened a drawer in his desk and removed long curved knife. He made his way around the desk and dropped to a knee, holding the knife an inch from Darren's face. It looked very sharp. "Now, Mr. Jenkins, we see if you're the type of person that does well with adversity."

"I'm your biggest fan," the blonde said. Her shirt was tight, the outline of her bra showing beneath the thin cotton. "I'm sure you hear that a lot." She tucked a curl behind her ear the way all young college girls do when they're nervous.

"It never gets old," Darren replied. His scribbled his name across the title page, as he had been doing for the last three hours. He flexed his hand afterwards and crossed his arms over the signature, leaning across the table to give her his biggest smile. "Say, would you like to get a drink later?"

She smiled and looked down at his arm resting on the table

before shaking her head. "No. No, that's okay. I just wanted you to know." She left, a little too quickly, and glanced back once.

"That was the last one, Mr. Jenkins," Nedry said. He hefted an unopened box of books like a kitten and tossed it on his shoulder. "Do you need help getting back to the hotel?"

"No, I'm okay. I think a little stroll would do me good, get the creative juices flowing before I hit the laptop later."

He nodded, and looked at his watch. "Remember, it's a Friday."

Darren laughed, "I know, I know. I've got your damn words already, big guy," he said, throwing a fake punch into Nedry's mid-section. "I want to finish this chapter before I hand it over. It's a bit of a cliff hanger and I think Mr. Nunziata will love it." Nedry rolled his eyes and left.

Darren took his time, walking around the bookstore, admiring the prominent display Mr. Nunziata had scored for his debut, the book already a critical darling. Mr. Nunziata was already haggling with Hollywood about the movie rights, and Darren was sure he would get a hand in writing the script.

"Did you write this?" a small voice asked from behind. A kid, no more than twelve, stood looking at Darren's photo on the back of the dust jacket of his book.

"Sure did," Darren said.

"I was going to buy a copy. For my mom. She loves these kind of books, with policemen on the cover."

Darren knelt down, "Well, tell you what. How about I sign it for you? You can tell her you met the author."

"Cool!" the kid said pushing the book towards Darren. He reached across his body and took it, tucking it under his arm so he could fumble for a pen. He caught the kid staring at his arm and knew what question would come next. "Does that hurt?" the kid asked.

Darren frowned. At least the kid had been raised well enough to keep from pointing. "No, not anymore. It just makes things harder." The distinct metal clink of a steel hook against the metal pen rose above the din of the patrons. A few heads turned to look and averted their eyes quickly, as if his disability were contagious. He scribbled his name and passed the book back. "Here you go, tell you mom I said thanks for reading."

"Thanks! I will." He scurried off to the register.

Darren left. He had decided to cut his stroll to the hotel short, hailing a cab outside the small, independent bookstore. It was already nine o'clock and he felt an intense need to finish the chapter and drop the pages by the door rise up in him like an unwelcomed ghost. He figured a thousand more words would do it. He stared at the steel hook attached to his wrist.

He was still under contract for another book, and a thousand words were a lot harder to come by these days.

THE END

About the Author: When he's not chained to the keyboard, TS Hall can be found slinging cardboard at the local comic book shop, or binge-watching horror movies on Netflix. Born and raised in the darkest parts of Appalachia, he now lives in Florence, Kentucky with his wife and three daughters. His writing can also be found in the Pebble Lake Review.

No Experience Necessary

Lorraine Nelson

Uma took A deep breath and knocked, hardly able to believe her luck. Twenty-five dollars an hour to babysit a kid? Who pays that kind of money? She shrugged. Who cares? She could easily make a hundred bucks tonight, and if the parents and the kid liked her, she could make that all summer long. It would be sweet to go into her senior year at Jefferson High with money already saved for college.

"Uma. Right on time. Come on in."

Uma smiled at the woman as she stepped inside, reminded again of mothers from old sitcoms on TV Land. The woman even wore a floral dress and had pearls around her neck. To complete the image, her auburn hair was piled high in a bun.

Uma followed her down the hallway, the sense of having stepped back in time growing stronger with every step. The place was overrun with lace and doilies, reminding Uma of her grandmother's condo.

"Katarina's looking forward to meeting you," Mrs. Smith said, her kitten heels clicking against the tile floor as she led the way down the dimly-lit hall.

"I can't wait to meet her," Uma said, quickening her pace to keep up. "It's too bad she was at band practice when I came for the interview on Wednesday."

"Yes. Well, here we are." She opened a set of double doors and stepped into a warm, cheerful family room.

"Katarina, dear. Look who's here," Mrs. Smith said.

The child was seated on the floor in front of a large flat-screen TV. She gave no indication of having heard her mother. Her eyes were fixed on the screen, her body rigid.

"Hello Katarina," Uma said, walking toward her.

No response.

Unsure of how to proceed, Uma glanced at the girl's mother, who stood by the doors with her hands pressed together.

"She's a little tired," the woman said softly. "She had a rough day at school. It's hard being the new child."

"Oh sure. I understand." She glanced at the kid, thinking that this was going to be a long night.

"Well, we'll be leaving now," Mrs. Smith said, looking at her watch. "We're going to the movies and then for a quick bite. We'll be gone two, three hours, tops."

"Take your time," Uma said, smiling at her. "We'll be fine."

"Okay then. Good luck." She turned to the girl. "Behave yourself Katarina. Remember what we talked about."

The child remained motionless. After a moment's hesitation, the woman turned to leave and shut the doors softly behind her.

Uma walked to Katarina and cleared her throat. The child turned to stare at her, her expression hostile. *Well, at least she's acknowledged me,* Uma thought. It's a start.

"So," Uma said, sitting cross-legged on the carpet beside Katarina. "How are you?"

Silence. The child continued to stare at her, and Uma noticed with a start that the child's eyes were so dark they appeared black. In that tiny white face, they looked like two black buttons. Like a doll's eyes. Dead. Empty.

Goosebumps peppered Uma's arms. She searched for something to say. Anything that would spark some life into those eyes. "How was band practice the other day?"

Katarina's gaze never wavered. "What band practice?"

"The one you were at when I came to meet your parents on Wednesday."

The child shook her head. "I don't have band practice. That's only for kids who play an instrument."

Uma frowned. "But your mom said…"

"May I have some lemonade, please?" Katarina's obsidian eyes held Uma's, but now they glittered with an intensity that further unnerved Uma.

"I don't understand. Why would your mom say you were at band practice if you don't play an instrument?"

Katarina turned back to the TV. "I don't want to talk about it anymore."

"But…"

"I said I'd like some lemonade. I'm thirsty."

Uma sighed, rising to her feet. She'd deal with this later. "Don't you think your mom would prefer that you drink milk instead?" she asked.

"We don't have any milk."

"Oh. Well, in that case, I'll get you some lemonade. Be right back, okay?"

At the door, she felt the skin on the back of her neck tingling and turned to find Katarina's gaze fixed on her. Uma smiled and exited the room quickly. She shut the doors behind her, leaned back against them, and took a deep breath.

Why would Mrs. Smith lie to her? It made no sense. Uma shook her head. Didn't matter anyway. Something was off about the kid. *One and done*, she thought. *They couldn't pay me enough to come back here.* Starting tomorrow, she'd look for a new summer job, like swabbing fishy entrails off the sidewalks down at the docks. Anything would be an improvement over babysitting this kid.

Her rubber soles made no noise as she walked toward the kitchen. The house was huge and full of dark corners and shadows. Uma shivered and quickened her pace. No wonder the kid acted weird. This house was eerie and would give anyone the willies.

A group of photos on a wall caught her attention. They were all of the family, with the parents smiling broadly, their warmth and friendliness shining through. But not Katarina. Creepy as she looked in the flesh, it was nothing compared to how downright scary she looked in the photos. Her small, sharp features stood out against the curtain of black hair framing her face, but it was her eyes that held Uma captive. Her expression in every photo was exactly the same. They burned with an unsettling ferocity, like a cornered animal. And they stared right at Uma.

Without thinking, Uma pulled out her phone and called Jen, her best friend.

"Hey, Jen."

"Hey, how's the job going?"

"The kid's weirding me out. I can't wait for the Smiths to get home so I can take off."

Jen laughed. "You're telling me you're afraid of a six-year-old kid?"

"You'd be freaked out too. I'm telling you, Jen, all she does is sit and stare at the TV. And the only time she spoke was to tell me that her mom lied to me about her being at band practice the other day."

Jen was quiet for a moment. "Okay," she finally said. "That makes no sense. The kid's yanking your chain."

"Maybe. Except…I dunno. She's kind of…creepy."

"Uma, she's six. Give her a break," Jen replied.

"Easy for you to say. You're not in this creepy old place," Uma said with a shudder.

"Oh, so now the kid and the house are creepy?" Asked Jen with a hint of amusement in her voice.

"Yeah. So?"

Jen laughed again. "Listen to yourself! Didn't I say you watch way too many horror flicks?"

"This isn't a horror movie, Jen."

"No, it's not. It's a babysitting job. Will you just relax and do your job and stop freaking out?"

"I'm not…" a soft, muffled thump made Uma jump. "Crap."

"What?"

"I just heard a sound upstairs."

"Maybe they have a cat. Or a dog," Jen offered.

"I'll call you back," Uma whispered and hung up. She stood silently, holding her breath. The quiet of the house enveloped her, squeezing her until she couldn't stand it any longer.

Taking a deep breath, she moved soundlessly to the main hallway and stared up at the grand staircase. The house was silent, save for the soft tick-tock of the grandfather's clock that stood against the far wall. The only other sound Uma heard was her own ragged breathing. *Jen's right,* she thought. *I'm letting the kid get to me.* With a final glance at the stairs, she turned and headed into the kitchen.

Uma looked around. "Wow," she muttered. "Some kitchen." It was bright and clean, with sparkling appliances that looked new.

Searching for glasses, she opened a cupboard and stared at nothing. The cupboard was completely empty. She tried another and found it empty as well. Puzzled, she threw open cupboard after cupboard, and then drawer after drawer, and all with the same disturbing result.

What the heck?

Uma stood in the center of the kitchen, breathing hard. She couldn't see a single dish, cup, or plate in the entire kitchen. She glanced at the shiny stovetop and opened the oven door. Brand new. The packaging material from the manufacturer was still inside.

Okay, so the Smiths had just redone their kitchen and hadn't had time to move back all the dishes and utensils. She'd just grab the lemonade and go. Strange, though, that they didn't mention anything to her. Sighing, Uma opened the fridge.

What the heck?

The fridge was empty, except for one lone bottle of lemonade on the top shelf. Uma gaped at the lemonade, then yanked open the freezer door, knowing what she'd see, but needing to check anyway.

Empty. She shut the freezer quickly.

Uma reached for the lemonade. As she straightened, she heard the sound again, a soft, muffled thud on the floor above her. She stood riveted, every sense tuned to the sound. Maybe Jen was right and there was a pet the Smiths hadn't told her about. She held her breath, waiting to hear something more. Anything. But silence reigned. Clutching the bottle of lemonade, she walked out of the kitchen.

As she passed the grand staircase, she heard the thud again. Then again. But this time, the thud was punctuated by a soft, rustling sound. Uma's head whipped around to the source. The rustling was coming from the curve in the staircase. Uma's breath caught in her throat. She waited, her heart rate accelerating as she listened.

As Uma watched, a pair of hands slid into view on the stairs. Transfixed, rooted in place, Uma watched as the hands edged their way down. I'm dreaming. It's just a dream, she thought, as a head slowly came into view around the bend.

The bottle of lemonade slipped from Uma's fingers, crashing to the floor. She barely noticed the spray of liquid and glass. Barely noticed anything, save the horror playing out before her.

Slithering down the stairs toward her like a white, fleshy, grotesque snake, was Mrs. Smith, her arms pulling her along, her red hair coiled on top of her head like a flaming crown. Her eyes were twin coals, blazing red-hot, and they glared at Uma. As Uma stared back, slack-jawed and light-headed, the woman's tongue darted out, and she licked her lips. She's getting her pretty dress all dirty, Uma thought and felt a crazy laugh bubble up inside her.

"Uma! Run!" Katarina's high-pitched shriek burst through Uma's paralysis, galvanizing her into action. She flew toward the family room, scooping the girl up with one arm and shutting the doors with the other.

"Help me," she whispered, setting the girl down and running toward the couch. Together they pushed the couch in front of the doors, just as something slammed into it.

"Mama! No!" Katarina screamed.

Uma backed up, her breathing hard and erratic. No time to panic. She grabbed a high-backed chair and threw it at the French windows. Then watched in horror as the chair bounced off the window.

"There's no way out," Katarina said, sounding young and helpless. "The glass doesn't break and the doors are locked." She tugged at Uma's jacket, looking up at her, eyes wide and imploring.

"I'm sorry," she whispered, her voice small and shaky, as she slipped her hand into Uma's. "Mama wouldn't let me warn you to stay away. That's why she wouldn't let me meet you the other day."

Uma's fingers closed around the tiny hand as she scanned the room for something to use as a weapon. Questions flooded her mind, but now was not the time to ask any of them.

There. The fireplace poker. Uma grabbed it and backed up slowly, pushing Katarina behind her.

"I'll hold her off," she whispered to the child. Her eyes remained fixed on the doors. "When I say so, I want you to run as fast as you can for the nearest neighbor, okay? Ask them to call the police." She looked at Katarina, who was watching her with wide, frightened eyes. "Can you do that, honey?"

Katarina nodded, her eyes filling with tears. "She'll kill you," she whispered, her breath catching.

Uma shook her head, her grip tightening on the poker as something slammed into the doors and rocked the couch.

"No, she won't. I won't let her. I just need you to do what I said. Okay?"

"Yes, I will. Promise you won't die like the others?"

Like the others? Oh God. What was going on in this house?

"Uma?" Katarina tugged on her shirt. "Promise." Her voice was so small, so full of fear.

A white-hot anger sizzled through Uma. How dare that witch frighten her own daughter so badly? Why wasn't she locked up somewhere? And why did I take this damn job?

"I promise," she said. She forced a smile. "Don't worry, okay? We'll be fine." She turned back to the doors. One more slam and they'd fly open.

"Get ready," Uma whispered, and held the poker out in front of her like a Samurai sword. Whatever this woman's issues were, Uma would inflict real damage before she would let anything happen to Katarina. The creepy little girl had turned into a victimized child, and Uma would protect the child no matter how batcrap crazy the mother was.

The doors burst open and Mrs. Smith entered the room on all fours, like a human spider. Her hands and feet made soft tapping noises as she padded forward with quick, jerky movements. Uma watched in fascinated horror as the woman lifted her head and sniffed the air. Then Mrs. Smith cocked her head toward Uma, and slowly got to her feet, smiling benignly. Her hair hung lopsided from its bun and her dress had dark smudges.

She looked from Uma to Katarina and back again. "Why Uma, my dear. Whatever are you doing with that poker? Put it down at once. Someone might get hurt."

"Go to hell, you...you freak," Uma snapped, pushing Katarina behind her and inching her way along the wall toward the doors.

The woman's eyebrows arched up. "Such language, and in front of my child. I'm afraid I'll have to lower your pay scale."

"Keep your friggin' money," Uma ground out. She kept sliding her feet, moving sideways. Behind her, Katarina kept pace.

"That's enough of that potty mouth," Mrs. Smith said sharply, her green eyes flashing. "Mr. Smith and I don't like bad language used in front of our child." She held out a hand. "Katarina, come to me. It's past your bedtime."

The child peeked out from behind Uma and shook her head.

"Katarina!" the woman said, her voice soft now, wheedling. Cajoling. "Mama wants to talk to Uma about grownup stuff and you need to go to bed."

"No!" the child said, clutching at Uma's jacket. "Mama, please. I want to stay with Uma."

The woman's eyes flew to Uma, who was still holding the poker in front of her. "What have you done to my child?"

Uma shook her head. "Me? I'm not the crazy psycho mother here. Now I know why she acted so weird. She's terrified of you. Can't you tell?"

The woman snarled, a ferocious animal sound that almost made Uma drop the poker. Behind her, Katarina whimpered.

Mrs. Smith took a step toward them, her eyes glittering with a cold fire. "Put the poker down, my dear. And we'll discuss this like ladies. You're upsetting Katarina."

Uma barked out a laugh. "I'm upsetting her? Lady, you slithered down the freaking stairs and scampered in here like a giant spider."

"I'm warning you, young lady. You don't know what you're dealing with. Put that down before I get upset." Her voice softened. "Because, trust me, you don't want to see me upset. You won't like me one little bit."

"I don't like you now," Uma snapped. *Just a few more steps. Just keep her talking.* "Perhaps if you explained why you want to hurt me, it'll change my impression of you."

Mrs. Smith laughed, a light lilting sound that belied the

malice in her eyes. "Hurt you? Why my dear, I don't want to hurt you. That was never my intention."

Uma frowned. "What is your intention?"

"I just need to feed on you. That's all. Since Katarina seems to have taken a shine to you, I'll even let you live instead of draining you dry." Her lips split in a macabre version of a smile.

Uma clutched the poker tightly, her fingers white against the shiny copper. "You're sick," she whispered. Another small step. Then another. "You need help."

A soft, throaty laugh escaped the woman's lips. "No, my dear girl. I need sustenance." Just as suddenly as it had come, the garish smile disappeared. "I'll give you one last chance to come to me willingly. Do it and you live. Defy me and I will drain you dry and toss your dried husk into the furnace."

"Nobody's feeding on me, with or without my permission." Out of the corner of her eye, Uma saw that they were near the doors. She and Mrs. Smith had completed a slow circle as they'd talked. It was now or never.

"Katarina! Go!" she screamed, gripping the poker in front of her for dear life.

The child didn't wait to be asked twice. She streaked out of the room as if all the demons of hell were after her.

"Katarina! Stop!" Her mother commanded, taking a step toward the doors. Uma swung the poker as if her very life depended on it.

The poker sliced neatly through the bodice of Mrs. Smith's dress, leaving a long, horizontal gash. The woman glanced down as if unable to believe what had just happened. Then she raised icy emerald eyes to Uma and snarled again. Only this time, she bared her fangs and lunged.

No, no, no, no, no! Uma's brain refused to accept what her eyes had just witnessed. She reacted automatically, swinging the poker again and again. Felt it make contact with the woman.... the thing....as it advanced toward her.

Uma couldn't give Mrs. Smith a chance to get closer, and she kept slashing, praying every swing would make contact.

Suddenly the poker was gone. Snatched from her hands.

Dazed, breathing so hard she could barely stand, she looked up. Mrs. Smith stood in front of her, the poker held casually in her hand. She bent her head toward Uma, laughing softly. Uma shrunk away, stumbling back against the wall.

"Silly little fool," the woman, or whatever it was, crooned. "Did you really think you could hold me off with a fireplace poker? I've been attacked by the best and worst of humanity. And none of them lived to tell of it. Did you really think that you, a puny girl, could stop me?"

"What—what are you?" Uma croaked. Was this it? Was this how she would die? Drained of blood by a monster and thrown into a fire? No one knowing what became of her? The thought of her parents' grief almost undid her. An image of her mother, in a white silk sari, sobbing into her father's shoulder, squeezed her chest so tight that she couldn't breathe. *Ma. Papaji. I'm so, so sorry.*

"What am I?" The woman-thing laughed. "Someone who's been here long before you came into this world, my dear. Someone who'll be here long after you leave." The hostility that had been in her eyes was now replaced by a look of ravenous hunger. Uma shivered.

"Please let me go," Uma whispered. "I won't tell anyone. I promise." Not true. If she got away, she'd alert the world in every way she could. People needed to know that monsters really do exist.

This particular one cocked its head. "Now we both know I can't do that. Comply, and I promise it'll be over fast. Struggle, and oh my dear, I swear you'll regret it."

"I'm not going to let you eat me," Uma screamed, her fingers closing around the vase on the side table. She swung it at the thing's head with all her might.

Uma didn't wait to see if it worked. She bolted for the

door and ran down the hallway. Behind her, the monster howled with rage, which propelled Uma toward the front door even faster. Sobbing, fumbling with the knob, she wrenched it open and stumbled into the night.

And slammed into something.

"My dear girl. Are you all right?"

Uma blinked. "Mr. Smith?" she whispered. Katarina was in his arms, her eyes wide, glistening with tears.

"Going somewhere, dear girl?" he said, smiling at her. His eyes blazed, red and hot as the fires of hell.

Uma's scream exploded into the night before everything went black.

THE END

About the Author: Global citizen. Lifelong writer. Voracious reader. Frequent traveler. Avid moviegoer. Geeky sci-fi fanatic. Lover of cupcakes.

Extra Small Medium

Kathryn Hearst

They say some babies are born with old souls. I don't know if that's true, because that would mean souls are reborn. In my experience, they sort of hang around girls like me.

My name is Jolene and I'm a medium. My momma calls me an extra-small medium as a joke. The first time I saw a soul, I was about two years old. I know they say you can't remember anything until you're three or four, but whoever "they" are—they're wrong.

"Why does she stare off like that?" Miss Roxy waved her hand a couple inches from my face.

I paid her no mind. I wanted to touch the blue ball of light over Roxy's head. It twinkled like a star, and I wanted to touch it. I climbed onto the couch, stretching as high as I could.

"I think she's just thinkin'." Momma pulled me into her lap. She knew I was special, even if other people thought I was slow. The doctor down at the clinic tested me for all sorts of things, but everything came back normal. Maybe Momma should have Miss Roxy tested for rudeness. I wonder if they made medicine to cure that.

I wiggled from my momma's arms and stood on the couch. I reached for the star again, but even on tippy-toe, I couldn't touch it. With all my might, I pulled myself onto the back of the couch. Momma started to pull me down.

No! I screamed inside my head. She couldn't hear me, but she got the idea when I wiggled and fussed.

I leaned against the wall and stood with my feet even with momma's head. This time, I brushed the star with my fingers. My fingers ached from the cold, and then the star burst like a bubble. It reformed across the room, well out of my reach.

"For heaven's sake, get that baby down from there before she falls." Roxy shook her head.

"Oh, my goodness. I didn't even notice…" Momma wrapped her hands around my middle and set me on the floor. I hated Miss Roxy, the next door neighbor. She's always been a busybody.

Momma said, "I entered Jolene in the 'Little Miss Cutie-Pie' contest. I got her a pretty pink dress at the thrift shop, and Dewitt is gonna' fix up the old wagon."

"Is he now? Just like he is supposed to fix the sink in the bathroom and mow the yard?" Roxy's lips twisted, making her ugly face uglier.

"Yes, he said he is gonna' paint it white and put pink roses on it, like a princess carriage." Momma's voice was full of pride. I liked her smile when she pushed my curls out of my eyes.

"Momma?" I climbed into her lap and set my hands on her cheeks. I had something important to say. "Gramma says, no cry."

"All right, Jo-Jo. Momma no cry."

Momma lied. She cried all the time. I knew daddy made her cry. He hurt her sometimes too, but he never hurt me.

I wandered into the kitchen to find Momma's phone. I needed to talk to my gramma, or she needed to talk to me. Her voice echoed through my head and wouldn't stop. "Okay Gramma. I loves you too."

I handed the phone to my Momma before it rang. "No cry."

She grinned and brought the phone to her ear. "Hello?" Her grin turned to a frown. "Yes, this is her."

Momma watched me. She looked scared, and I wondered

if she was afraid of me.

"I will be right there. Thank you."

Miss Roxy stood and gave me a dirty look, then turned to Momma. "What is it?"

"My mom, she had a heart attack. They said I need to get to the hospital, she is on life-support." Momma wiped the tears from her cheeks.

"Jesus, Mary and Joseph! Jo-Jo told you her gramma said not to cry. She's been talking about her all morning." Miss Roxy looked as if she wanted to run away. "She's like that New York lady with the big white hair! She talks to dead people."

"Stop it. My mother isn't dead."

I'll never forget the fear in her eyes when she picked me up and handed me to Miss Roxy. I knew I'd done something wrong, though I didn't understand what.

"Jolene, hurry up and get dressed; you are gonna' miss the bus!" Momma yelled. I think her nerves were worse than mine.

The first day of fourth grade at a new school. Momma said I needed a fresh start. I'd scared the heck out of my third grade teacher when I told her that her husband's wedding ring was in a coffee can in the garage. Sure enough, Mrs. Heekin found the ring in a rusted can filled with nails and screws. It had been missing for nearly two years before Mr. Heekin died.

Needless to say, she had other things to discuss at the parent teacher conference than my trouble with math. After an hour of me giving the teacher messages from beyond the grave, Momma decided to look for a new school.

We couldn't afford Tuskawilla Preparatory Academy, but I attended on a full scholarship, courtesy of the State of Florida. They called me "special needs" in kindergarten. I was diagnosed with Attention Defect Disorder in second grade, and in third they labeled me with "troubled."

According to the school counselor, the public school system couldn't meet my needs, but I thought they met my needs just fine with their special classes. The truth of it stung—they didn't want me at their school.

The lady offered to fill out my scholarship application the same day I gave her a message from her dead brother. That day I developed a new appreciation for my gift.

"Jolene, I thought I told you to make up your bed?" Momma stepped over toys and books, to collect dirty clothing. Shelves of pageant trophies lined one wall of my tiny bedroom, some as tall as me.

"I don't want to go to a new school. I hate this stupid uniform. Why can't I go to the old school?" I closed my eyes tight and screwed up my face. I tried to stop my tears, it didn't work.

"It's a nice school, Jo-Jo. Give it a chance." Momma set the laundry basket on the bed and hugged me. "Remember, no talkin' to ghosts at school. People don't like it when you tell them about their dead kin-folk."

"I can't help it if they talk to me." I wiped my nose on the back of my hand, and marched into the kitchen to grab a pop-tart.

"That isn't a proper breakfast."

"The bus is coming." I stepped out the door with the souls in my head telling me to run or I'd miss it.

The bus was unlike any I'd ever ridden. It had cloth seats and seatbelts for each of the students. My stop was the last on the route so the only empty seat was in the front row.

Everyone chatted about the first day, everyone except the little boy beside me. He wore the same khaki shorts and navy blue polo as me, but instead of white ankle socks and dress shoes, he wore white tube socks with blue stripes at the top, and beat up Nikes.

"Hi. I'm Jolene." I offered the kid half of my pop-tart.

"My name is Thomas." He mumbled and glanced nervously at the bus driver. He shook his head and pointed to the "No Food or Drinks" sign.

My stomach rumbled as I stuffed my breakfast back into

my bag. I usually ate free breakfast at my old school. The fancy new school didn't have a cafeteria. In the corner of my mind the souls called my name. I stared straight ahead, determined to ignore them.

The ride to school took forever. The longer we rode, the louder the others talked—both the students and the ghosts.

A female soul asked me to speak to Chelsea. A man asked me to find Brittany. Still another, softer voice asked for Tommy. I eyed the little kid beside me, and shook my head. Nope, no way was I going to mess up at another school.

Jolene, Tommy is my little boy. Tell him his mommy loves him. Please, tell him I'm sorry I had to go.

I folded my arms and closed my eyes tight. "No."

Tommy scooted away from me.

Jolene, please tell him I miss him. Tell him his bunny isn't lost. It's under the seat in the car. Tommy's mother sounded so sad, I had to help.

I leaned close to him. "This is gonna sound weird, but I can talk to people in heaven. Your momma, she's dead?"

Tommy hung his head. "Yeah."

"She says she loves you and misses you."

"That's not funny. It's not nice to tease people," he shrieked.

"She says your bunny is under the seat in the car."

Tommy's wails drew the attention of the bus driver.

The driver narrowed her eyes at me in the mirror. "You there. No talking until we get to school. You should be ashamed of yourself for picking on someone younger than you."

"I'm sorry." I curled into myself and fought back tears.

I made my way to my classroom. My backpack hung all the way to the backs of my knees. It was packed full of crayons, pencils, tissues, hand sanitizer and other stuff. It felt like I carried half of Walmart. The backpack hit the floor with a loud thump, and everyone turned and stared.

"Good morning, Jolene." The teacher smiled.

I couldn't remember the teacher's name and blushed deep red.

Kitty Cat. A male soul spoke in my head.

It popped out of my mouth before I could stop it. "Good morning, Miss Kitty Cat."

The room erupted in giggles, but the teacher wasn't smiling. She stared with the same wide-eyed expression that all adults had when I repeated something from a ghost.

My teacher, Ms. Cathleen Jenkins, shook her head and forced a smile. "It's okay, my father used to call me that when I was a little girl. I prefer Ms. Jenkins now."

The other students giggled when I sat at my desk. A dark haired girl mocked my southern drawl while repeating "Ms. Kitty Cat". I guess kids from the other side of town didn't talk like country folk. Five other girls circled the dark haired one, laughing hysterically. I didn't dare turn around.

We ate lunch in the cafeteria, but no one talked to me. Ms. Jenkins must have felt sorry for me, because she sat at my desk—which only made things worse.

The other girls continued to make fun of my accent and my no-name shoes. The words "new girl" and "scholarship" were whispered like dirty words. I wanted to crawl under the table.

I'd never felt so alone.

When I was upset, the souls roared to life. Sometimes they offered advice, sometimes a kind word, and other times they all spoke at once. I put my hands to my ears and rocked back and forth in my chair. I'd learned a long time ago nothing could drown out a sound inside my brain, but sometimes rocking would calm me down.

I closed my eyes as tightly as I could and gritted my teeth. Ms. Jenkins asked if I was all right. I couldn't answer. The voices grew louder and things crashed to the floor. I opened my eyes, shocked to see that every book in the classroom library had fallen. The kids in the classroom shouted, some were frightened; others laughed.

"All right, everyone calm down. I am going to send you to recess early today. Can I have two volunteers to stay and help clean up the mess?" Ms. Jenkins seemed a little nervous; two wrinkles made an eleven between her eye brows. Courtney raised her hand, and five additional hands popped up. I also raised my hand, after all, I'd caused the mess.

"Jolene and Courtney may stay to help clean up, everyone else… enjoy your recess."

Courtney and I eyed each other.

Ms. Jenkins said, "Courtney, why don't you introduce yourself?"

"My name is Courtney Louise McNamara." She pushed her dark hair off one shoulder and set her hands on her hips.

"I'm Jolene Parks."

Courtney's eyes twinkled, and a smile tugged at the corners of her mean little mouth. "Parks?"

Ms. Jenkins went to her desk to eat her lunch while we worked. By the end of the day I had no friends and a new nick name, "Jolene Trailer Parks." Courtney harassed me until she had to leave school early because of a splitting head ache. Strangely enough, the souls quieted after Courtney left.

My tap number went off perfectly. I'd never performed so well in front of people. I felt like I cheated a little, because one soul counted while another reminded me of the steps. I curtsied three times before the applause settled down, and I left the stage. For once, I didn't mind the extra people in my head.

Momma smiled and whisked me off to the dressing room. I had a few minutes to change into my next costume.

"You rocked it baby!" Momma gave me a high five and pulled out a fluffy white dress. Between the sequins and ruffles, it weighed almost as much as me.

"I'm gonna come in second, Momma. They told me." I tugged the dress up to my shoulders.

"Did they say who was gonna' win?" Momma zipped the gown.

"Maelynn," I whispered.

"Hmm. Well do your best baby." Momma smiled.

I knew she smiled for my sake. The winner of the pageant would walk away with two thousand dollars, the chance to compete for a state title, and another eight grand in cash. That kind of money would help pay the rent. Maybe then Daddy would stop fussing about spending money on my pageants.

"Don't worry, Momma. The ghosts will fix it."

"What do you mean?" Momma looked around. I'd made her nervous.

"They told me they would make sure we win."

A short while later, there was a commotion on the other side of the room. Maelynn cried and squirmed around like a kitten stuck in a pillow case. Her mother tried to calm her down, but the little red-haired girl kept scratching until her dress tore. Momma watched the entire mess with sad eyes. I smiled and did my best to ignore Maelynn.

The beauty round of the Little Miss Orlando pageant ended, and I stood with the finalists onstage. One after another accepted their trophies, until only me and a swollen-faced Maelynn remained. Poor Maelyn couldn't stop squirming. She'd scratched and wiggled her way through the entire round. I swallowed back a lump in my throat, not because Maelynn was about to lose, but because I knew I would win. I wanted that crown, and the voices in my head told me I deserved it.

The following Monday, I stuffed the enormous crown into my backpack. I might not have the right kind of shoes, or come from the nice part of town, but I'd won a regional pageant. In a month, I'd take a whole week off school to go to the Little Miss Florida competition.

I sat next to Tommy on the bus. He reached into his bag and pulled out a stuffed rabbit.

"Can you tell my mommy I said thank you?"

I nodded. "She heard you."

"Jolene, you're my best friend." He took my hand and held it.

I didn't want anyone in my grade to see me holding his hand, but I didn't have the heart to stop him. I couldn't imagine losing my momma. Then again, I'd never really lose her. She'd always be with me, talking in my brain.

Despite holding hands with a first grader on the bus, this was the best day ever. I couldn't wait for the bell to ring and class to start. Ms. Jenkins always did Show and Tell on Monday mornings. Today was the first time I'd brought something to show the class.

"Who would like to go first this morning?" Ms. Jenkins asked with her usual smile. Two hands rose before she had finished the question. Of course, Courtney raised her hand too.

"Jolene, you may go first," Ms. Jenkins said.

I carefully pulled my rhinestone covered crown and walked to the front of the class. I held the crown so the class could see it. "My Show and Tell is that I won the Little Miss Orlando pageant on Saturday. Now I get to go to Tallahassee and try to win Little Miss Florida."

Several of the students gasped and whispered, but Courtney started the round of applause. Even Ms. Jenkins looked surprised that Courtney was being so nice to me. I curtsied and took a step back toward my desk.

"Time to pass the Show and Tell around to the class!" Courtney called from her desk in the back of the room.

I didn't know what to do. I didn't want to pass my crown around, but those were the rules. I looked toward the teacher for directions.

Ms. Jenkins shook her head. "You don't have to pass it around. It looks very delicate."

I looked over the class, everyone smiled, even Courtney. Why not pass it around? I'd earned it… well mostly. I carefully handed the crown to Michael in the first seat of the first row, and returned to my desk. Another student came to the front of the class, to share a shark's tooth he found at the springs.

I slid into my chair, still smiling. I'd be popular now. I might even be queen bee of the class.

"Oh no!" Someone called from the back of the classroom. One of Courtney's followers held part of the crown in her hand, a broken piece glimmered from the floor, and Courtney held a third piece in her hand.

"She dropped it and I tried to catch it, then it broke," Courtney said.

I knew she lied. I knew before the souls told me. I hated her. The girls had twisted my crown back and forth between them until it snapped into three pieces.

Ms. Jenkins said, "The metal band wouldn't have broken by falling on the carpet."

"It's just a cheap costume crown. She didn't win any pageant," Courtney said.

I didn't bother to try to close my eyes and keep my tears inside. "She did it on purpose."

"Girls, bring the pieces to me now." Ms. Jenkins ordered. She sounded as angry as the souls. She put her hand on my shoulder. I knew she wanted to help me, but I was too upset.

Chelsea walked up the aisle slowly. She looked as if she might cry too. I doubted she'd ever been in trouble. I hoped her daddy would whip her butt good when she got home.

Chelsea set the broken piece of crown into Ms. Jenkins hand. "I'm sorry."

Courtney took her sweet time coming forward. She stood with her hand clenched tightly around the broken crown, and moved to pick up the third piece. Somehow, her left foot caught the back leg of her chair. She stumbled and took the chair down with her.

Twenty-two sets of eyes watched as Courtney fell face first into the sharp, jagged piece of my crown. Time sort of stood still. It seemed like hours before the screaming started. The rhinestone covered metal jutted from Courtney's eye, and blood poured down her left cheek.

Pandemonium broke out in the classroom.

The remainder of fourth grade went by much easier for me. After Courtney returned to school with an eye patch, her friends ignored her. By the end of the year, I'd caught up with my grades. I had help from my souls, but not even Ms. Jenkins suspected me of cheating.

I hid under my bed when the fighting started. My momma and daddy fought often, but lately they fought with their hands. Mostly, they fought about me. Daddy didn't approve of the money Momma spent on my pageants. Costumes, entry fees and dance classes cost more than the rent, and they couldn't afford it. Momma argued that I'd won more money in the pageants than she'd spent.

Momma was right. I'd won Little Miss Florida and would move on to Little Miss USA. The cash prize was enough to put a down payment on a real house. I don't think Daddy cared much about the money. The ghosts told me to lock my doors at night. They didn't like the way he looked at me. I didn't like the way he looked at me either. He told me once that he didn't like his little girl becoming a woman. I wasn't even ten years old. How could I be a woman?

The screaming and yelling scared me, but I hated it when my momma cried in pain. I knew what it sounded like when a fist hit someone, and Daddy was definitely hitting Momma.

Daddy always had a drink in his hand. I knew enough to stay away from him when he was drunk. I wished Momma knew how to stay away from him too. That night, I begged her to stay with me, but she wouldn't.

I heard the punch, then everything went quiet. The souls told me to hold my breath and count. I made it to fifty before footsteps came up the hallway.

"Who is coming?" I asked the ghosts.

It's him. Stay still, they replied.

A cold ball of fear formed in my belly. Would he beat me too?

My bedroom door opened, and his boots moved around the edge of my bed.

"Come here Jolene." His words blurred together, like he had too much caramel in his mouth.

I drew every ounce of courage I had and scrambled out from under the bed. I couldn't make myself look at his face. The smells of stale beer and cigarettes made my belly clench. The souls spoke to me softly, telling me to stay calm, not to cry. I wanted to do as they said, but they were just ghosts, they couldn't keep me from getting a beating. Could they?

He held a pair of scissors in his hand. My mouth went dry. I knew better than to ask why he had the scissors. I bowed my head and slumped my shoulders. I wanted to make myself small, too small to hurt. He moved toward me and grabbed a handful of my hair.

"No! Please, no, Daddy, don't!" I screamed, begging him.

He wouldn't listen. He tightened his grip. I thought he would pull my hair out of my head instead of cut it. His fingers tightened on the scissors, but he didn't raise them.

Daddy grunted, and I tried to look up to see why. He shoved me backward and I fell to the floor. The hand holding the scissors shook. His eyes went wide and he shook his head like a crazy person.

"Daddy?"

"What the hell are you doing to me?" His eyes bulged out of his head like Miss Roxy's pug.

I scrambled to my feet and pressed my back against the wall. The scissors rose slowly to his chest. He fought to stop his hand, but his muscles and his brain were doing different things. The souls were making Daddy hurt himself, just like they made Courtney fall and Maelynn itch.

They shouted at me to run away, but I couldn't move. Then I heard her voice. Momma told me to go next door to Miss Roxy's trailer. I looked for her, but she was in my room. She spoke to me inside my head.

"Momma!" I didn't want her in my head. I needed her

for real.

Go now, baby, she said.

"I can't! He will hit me!" I screamed.

As soon as I said the words, Daddy took a couple of Frankenstein steps toward me.

My legs began to move and before I knew it, I ran out the trailer. I beat on Miss Roxy's door until my hands went numb. "Help, please, help."

Miss Roxy opened the door. "What in the hell? Jolene, are you…"

A scream burst out of my trailer; a deep sound of a man in pain. Me and Miss Roxy turned toward my front door. I expected Daddy to come crashing through any minute, but he never did.

Miss Roxy pushed me into her house and locked the door. "What happened? Where's your momma and daddy?"

I started to answer her, but then another familiar voice spoke to me.

I'm right here, Daddy whispered from heaven or the other place, I didn't know which.

"They're dead."

THE END

About the Author: Kathryn M. Hearst is a southern girl with a love of the dark and strange. Besides writing, she has a passion for shoes, vintage clothing, antique British cars, music, musicians and all things musical (including theatre). Kate lives in central Florida with her chocolate lab, Jolene; and two rescue pups, Jagger and Roxanne. Her short stories have been published in various anthologies. Her debut novel, Feast of the Epiphany, will be out in June 2016, followed by The Spirit Tree and Feast of Mercy Fall 2016. www.kathrynmhearst.com

MOUNTAIN OF THE LOST

SHANNON HOLLINGER

The girls left the safety of the car and stared up at their goal from the parking lot. The mountain loomed high above them, its peak concealed behind a thick layer of fog. Crossing the dirt lot, the three girls paused at the bulletin board at the foot of the trail and looked at the map.

"Which way are we taking?" Brittany turned to look at the mountain again.

"That one." Kate pointed. "The Beckman's Trail. The steepest, most direct way to the summit."

"Is that really necessary?"

"I thought you wanted a challenge?"

"Will you guys look at this?" Lisa gestured to a weathered flyer posted to the end of the board. They gathered around the faded paper, squinting to make out the text. "She was almost our age. She's been missing for three months," Lisa said softly.

"What kind of a sixteen-year-old girl goes out to hike a mountain alone?" Brittany asked. "Better yet, what kind of parents let their daughter go do something stupid like that? You ask me, she took off with some guy. That seems more likely, don't you think?"

"Maybe," Kate said absently, distracted as she tried to interpret the writing at the bottom of the flyer which had been smeared into hieroglyphs.

"Well, what else do you think could have happened?" Brittany scowled at Kate with narrowed eyes, arms crossed.

"You don't think she died up there, do you?" Lisa asked,

turning to Kate for an answer.

Kate met her eyes. She couldn't lie. "It's possible. I mean, it happens."

"No it doesn't," Brittany said.

"It does. Mostly in the winter, to people hiking in snow, but it does happen. It's a mountain. Sometimes people don't come down the way they'd like. Or at all, I guess."

"So if it's dangerous, why are we doing it?" Brittany asked.

"I thought it would be fun," Lisa said. "So did Kate."

Kate didn't respond, transfixed by the picture of a lost girl named Gabby with long red hair.

"Well, we're never going to even get started unless everyone shuts up and gets moving," Brittany said.

The girls adjusted their packs and headed for the trailhead, each casting a last look at the washed out picture of a young girl who had vanished on the same mountain they were about to climb.

They hiked in silence, lost in their own thoughts as they labored towards the summit. They were soon winded, panting from the exertion of the hike. They paused at a fork in the trail, using the opportunity to catch their breath and grab some water from their packs. Kate pulled a map out of her pocket, consulting it before continuing on, leading the way up the trail to their left. They gasped as their bodies fought to acclimate to the thinning air and the effort of the hike, climbing higher with each step, every stride bringing them closer to their goal. Another hour in, they came upon a boulder blocking their way.

"Let's take a break," Kate said as she studied the huge rock before them.

Brittany and Lisa both nodded, quickly taking off their packs and doing their best to sip their water slowly. Kate left her pack on the side of the trail as she explored their options, paying close attention to the telltale marks left behind by trekking sticks from previous hikers.

"It looks like the only way past it is to climb over it," she finally concluded, breaking the news to the others.

"What the... how?" Brittany asked, crossing her arms as

she glared at the rock.

"Teamwork." Kate grinned as she pointed out the hand and toe holds they'd have to use to traverse the boulder.

Brittany rolled her eyes but donned her pack.

"I don't want to go first. Or last," Lisa said.

"I'll go first," Kate volunteered. "You can watch what I do."

She strapped her pack on and approached the obstacle with determination. Placing her foot on a narrow indent, she pushed off with her other leg, reaching for a small protrusion she saw above. Kate had scrambled her way to the top of the rock within minutes.

"Now you," she called down to Lisa. "It's not that hard, just stay close to the rock and keep your momentum going."

Lisa hesitantly put her foot on the rock. Swallowing her anxiety, she began climbing. She was almost at the top when she couldn't see where to go next. "Kate." Lisa's voice was shaky. "Kate, I can't see my next move."

"Hold on," Kate called from above. Her face appeared as she lay flat and looked over the edge of the rock. "You're going to have to raise your right foot, there's a notch around the level of your knee, and when you find that, push off and reach with your left, there's a crevice about a foot and a half above your right hand."

"Where?" Lisa stretched back, straining to see.

"No, Lisa, stay flat. Lisa, stay flat," Kate's voice rose as she realized what was going to happen, louder as she watched it happen. "Shit! Lisa! Lisa?" she called as Lisa lost her grip, sliding at first, then falling backwards through open space, crashing pack first through the brush below as she fell from sight.

"Lisa?" Kate called again as she scrambled back down the rock as quickly as she safely could. "Brittany, can you see her?"

"No, the brush is too thick." Brittany's voice was wavering. "Lisa?"

Back on the trail, Kate parted the brush at the base of the rock, trying to see where Lisa had fallen.

"I'm okay," Lisa called from below.

Kate and Brittany exchanged relieved looks.

"Just got the wind knocked out of me."

"What does it look like from down there?" Kate asked. "Is it safe for us to come down?"

"It's steep, but there are lots of roots. I might be able to climb back up."

"No, wait there, we need to come down and check you out first." Kate put her hand on Brittany's arm as the other girl rolled her eyes. "She could have a serious injury and not be feeling it from the adrenaline rush," she said in a low tone.

Brittany nodded her understanding and the two girls fought their way through the vegetation, lowering themselves backwards over the ledge of the path. Lisa was standing by the time they'd made their way down.

"What is this, another trail?" Brittany asked, looking around.

"Looks like it," Lisa nodded.

"It doesn't see much traffic, huh?" Brittany looked at the overgrowth that intruded on the thin grey line snaking its way through the brush. "And your sunglasses are totaled," she said as she bent to retrieve the mangled piece of eyewear from behind Lisa's feet.

"Those aren't mine," Lisa said, taking them from Brittany. "They look like they've been here for a while."

"You're not kidding."

Cakes of dirt fell from a shattered lens. Lisa tossed them back to the ground.

"This path isn't on the map," Kate said.

"It has to be." Brittany snatched the map from Kate to look for herself.

"But it's not," Kate said, tapping the trail with the toe of her boot as she waited for Brittany to come to the same conclusion.

"You're right," Brittany agreed. "You think it's a game trail?"

"No, I don't." Kate inspected the branches on the trees that lined the path. "Someone bushwhacked it. A few times.

You can see different ages in the damaged ends."

"Why?" Lisa asked.

"How would I know? Obviously to get to somewhere. We'll never know where unless we follow it for a bit," Kate said, raising her eyebrows.

Lisa and Brittany looked at each other. Brittany nodded to Lisa.

"Let's do it," Lisa said.

"You're sure you're alright?" Kate asked her.

"I'm fine. Luckily I landed on my butt."

"Plenty of cushioning there," Brittany joked.

Kate grabbed a broken branch the length of her leg from beside the trail and dug it firmly into the ground in the middle of the path as a marker for their return. Taking a long look to each side, she chose a direction and led the way.

"Do you think those sunglasses might have belonged to the missing girl?" Lisa asked, breaking the silence. No one answered. "Maybe she fell like I did. She might have hit her head, been disoriented and just started walking."

"Maybe," Kate said distractedly.

"You don't think we're going to find her body, do you?"

"Maybe. Maybe we'll find her still alive and she'll be ravenously hungry and turn cannibal on us," Brittany joked.

Lisa was quiet for a few minutes as they made their way farther up the path. "I don't want to do this anymore, you guys," she said. "I want to go back."

"God, you're such a baby," Brittany told her.

"And you're such a bitch," Lisa returned.

"I'd rather be a bitch than a sniveling, whining little..."

"Will you both just stop," Kate said, turning to face them. "You're both brats, and if I wanted to spend my day with a brat I would have stayed home and babysat my little brother. Besides, we're at the end, anyway."

The other girls looked up, noticing for the first time that the trail indeed ended in a rocky wall ahead of them.

"Well that sucks," Brittany said. "What's the point of a trail that leads to a dead end?"

Kate was inspecting the ground at the base of the escarpment. A drift of sand fell from a ledge, drawing her attention. Save for that she would have missed it. There was a gap low in the rocks off to the side, an opening more than big enough for a human to fit through should they notice the spot. She lowered herself to her knees, took off her pack and retrieved her flashlight. Adjusting the beam, she stuck her head inside the cave.

"What do you see?" Brittany asked.

"I can't tell. It looks like it opens into a big cavern. I'm going in."

"Be careful," Lisa warned as Kate's slender form disappeared into the mountain. She and Brittany crowded around the edge, looking in after Kate.

"I'm going in too," Brittany said, impatiently grabbing a flashlight from her pack and ducking through the crevice after Kate.

Not wanting to be left out, Lisa reluctantly followed suit.

Kate was surprised how dark and cold it was inside. The girls' three lights did little to illuminate the depths of the cavern, revealing only what the beams were directly focused on.

"Wow," Brittany said, spinning in a circle. The cave extended as far as she could see. Sharp tipped stalactites hung from the vaulted stone overhead menacingly, like fangs in the mouth of a beast. "This is incredible. Are you sure it wasn't on the map?"

"Positive," Kate said. Something about the space was giving her an eerie feeling. The hair on the back of her neck tickled as it rose, a rudimentary signal of alarm long forgotten over the course of evolutionary development. Kate had never experienced it before, but she recognized it for what it was - a warning of danger.

"Let's go," Kate said quickly, trying to wrangle her friends out of the dark space and back out into the daylight.

"No way," Brittany said. "We've got to check this out."

"We'll come back; now's not the time," Kate said, a growing sense of dread developing as she began to zero in on what her body was telling her.

"What's the rush?" Brittany asked, playing her beam along the walls around them.

"I don't think we're alone," Kate said.

"Don't be ridiculous," Brittany scoffed. Her light landed on a face. The teeth were bared in a frozen scream, sinew tight against the skull, eye orbs not quite empty. She screamed, the flashlight falling to the ground, the beam shakily illuminating the bound legs of the corpse as it rolled across the floor, landing against Kate's foot. Kate snatched the light up and focused it on the skull once again. The locks of red hair still framing the mummified face left no doubt as to the identity of the body.

"We found her," Lisa whispered, clutching at Kate's back as she peeked at the cadaver from around Kate's shoulder. Brittany calmed herself enough to join the huddle. Kate moved the light, playing the beam over the wrists, which had been bound so tight that even with the flesh dried and dehydrated the bonds were still snug. A chain linked the wrists to the ankles, the remaining length fading off beyond the boundary of the weak light. The body was adorned by a frilly pink dress, the kind a little girl might wear to a fancy party. Lace edged socks poked out of shiny black shoes. Remnants of garish make-up could be seen on the dried flesh.

Kate's gut told her this wasn't the danger they needed to fear. She felt a malevolent presence in the cave with them. Reaching down, she locked a hand around the other girls' wrists and started backing out of the cave.

"But..." Lisa started.

"Go." Something in Kate's hushed tone was enough to motivate both girls. They turned, rushing out through the narrow mouth of the cave, back into the blinding daylight. Kate followed slowly, unwilling to turn her back on whatever it was that lurked within the cavern. Blinking against the harsh glare of the sun, she grabbed her pack from the dirt next to the cave's entrance.

"I think someone was in there with us," she said, still

watching the opening.

"Why do you say that?" Lisa asked.

"I'm not entirely sure. Something just felt... evil. We need to get out of here. Fast."

"But what about..." Lisa started.

"We can come back later, with the cops. But we need to go."

"You don't have to tell me twice." Brittany started down the trail at a brisk pace. Kate gestured for Lisa to follow.

"No, you go first, you'll recognize the branch you left as a trail marker. I'll just knock it over without noticing."

Kate wanted to argue, but started after Brittany instead, jogging a few steps to close the distance. She wanted off the mountain. Now.

They rushed in hurried silence, no one wanting to discuss what they'd seen. Or the danger they might be in. The sun dropped behind the trees, long shadows falling around them in a sinister dance.

"Wait," Kate called to Brittany, grabbing her arm. "We should have reached the marker by now." Kate turned in a circle to orient herself. "Where's Lisa?" she asked, panic creeping around the sharp edge of her voice.

"I don't know; I thought she was behind you," Brittany said.

"She was." Kate trotted a few feet back down the trail. She could see nothing along the visible length of the pass.

"That's just like her," Brittany whispered. She cleared her throat, spoke louder. "She's probably curled up in the bushes somewhere, having a breakdown."

Kate gave her a look that told her to not start. "Well, we can't just leave her. And I swear we missed the marker." She squeezed past Brittany, looking at the path ahead of her. "There're no footprints down here. We did miss it. So we have to backtrack anyways."

Brittany nodded.

"Keep a lookout for where we came down. The stick, disturbed brush, heavy foot prints on the path... it's got to be here somewhere."

"What if we find the way back up before we find Lisa?"

"I don't know." Kate shook her head. "Let's just try to find them both."

Kate led the way, her eyes searching in every direction for some sign of familiarity. She stopped suddenly in the path, Brittany bumping into her from behind.

"What?" Brittany whispered. She clutched at Kate's arm.

"The trail's been wiped," Kate whispered back.

"What?"

"The trail. Our footprints. There's no sign of them."

Brittany looked at her blankly.

"Someone's erased our footprints from the path."

Brittany inspected the trail for herself, her eyes widening as she realized Kate was right.

"Oh God, Lisa," Kate said softly, reaching for Brittany's hand.

"What are we going to do?"

"I'm not sure." Kate took a long look in both directions. "Do you think we're better off looking for the spot where we climbed down from the main trail, or staying on this path and putting as much distance between us and the cave as possible?"

"This path. Let's keep moving," Brittany said, pulling her forward. "We've got to get out of here."

The two girls rushed along the trail holding hands, casting frequent glances behind them.

"This isn't right," Kate said, pausing. Brittany stopped, looking at her. "We can't leave. We've got to find Lisa. We can't just leave without knowing what happened to her."

"But Kate, what if she's... we can't go back. We don't even know..." Brittany's face contorted, her eyes bulging as her voice withered to a single squeak. She slowly bent her head, looking down. Kate followed her gaze; saw the tip of the arrow protruding from a splash of red that had flowered on the chest of Brittany's shirt like a rose in bloom.

Tears sprang to Kate's eyes. Her heart spasmed in her chest as her friend squeezed her hand tightly, looking at her with confusion in her eyes as she sank to her knees. Feeling exposed, Kate knew she had to run, had to take action if she were to survive. "I'm sorry," she cried as she let go of Brittany's hand, leaving her friend to hemorrhage by herself. "So sorry," she whispered as she stumbled back a few steps.

Kate looked past Brittany, searching for any signs of her assailant. Then she forced herself to turn around and run. She raced down the trail, looking for a break in the growth, watching for an opportunity to enter the woods. Tripping over a rope drawn across the trail, Kate was flying through the air before she even realized she had missed a step.

Kate awoke on her side. She was chilled so deeply that her bones ached. Struggling to sit up, a muscle in her back went into spasm, the pain radiating throughout her small frame. Her head throbbed with each beat of her pulse, a blinding pain that produced grey spots in her vision. She stopped struggling, laying still as she ran a mental inventory on her body.

She was slumped on her right side, her weight balanced painfully on her shoulder, hands bound tightly behind her back at the wrists. There were two sources of pain on her head. Her forehead above her right temple ached under the weight of her skull, the ground beneath it cold and hard. A tightness on her other brow hinted at a contusion.

Realizing she was in the cave, Kate froze. Candlelight threw the interior into layers of shadow beyond a small halo of visibility. She fought against the pain, straining to see as much as she could in her peripheral vision. The corpse was to her left. Kate swallowed a whimper as she realized she and her friends had just become members of the missing, faces on a sheet of paper posted to random bulletin boards and telephone poles. The feeble lighting dimmed as someone crossed between her and the candle.

"You're awake," Lisa said, crouching down in front of her.

"Oh my God, Lisa, you're okay." Words and tears rushed forth. "We've got to get out of here."

Lisa grabbed Kate by the shoulders and moved her into an upright position. "Why would we do that?"

Kate stared at her friend. There was a strange glaze in Lisa's eyes. Suspecting that she may have been drugged, Kate asked, "Who else is here with us? Have you seen Brittany?"

Wrinkling her nose, Lisa answered, "No, she wasn't invited. I don't like her. She's no fun to play with."

Kate's mind raced. It had been Lisa's idea to climb this mountain, Lisa who had pointed out the flyer of the missing girl, Lisa who had fallen off the main path onto the side trail with the cave and its horrible secret. Her brain fought against the obvious, struggled against what it all meant. She knew she needed to proceed with caution.

"You're right," Kate said as enthusiastically as she could. "What are we going to play?"

Lisa's face lit up. "I thought we'd start with a make-over. I'll do your hair and make-up first. Then we'll pick out something for you to wear. And then we'll move on to tea."

"That sounds like fun!"

"Oh, it will be. I've been thinking about your hair. I don't like it as long as it is now. I think we should cut it."

Kate felt Lisa's eyes focused on her. "You know what," she said, thinking of an answer. "You're right! I've been thinking the exact same thing myself."

Lisa's smile disappeared, her lower lip jutting out in an angry pout. "The haircut was my idea."

"Yes, of course it was," Kate said soothingly. "But as soon as you said it, I knew you were right. You're so good at these things."

Lisa's mood instantly shifted, a childlike grin on her face. She stood, talking over her shoulder as she walked deep into the dark recess of the cavern. "Wait until you see what I have."

Kate used the opportunity to test her bonds. The rope around her wrists and ankles was tied tight, biting into her flesh. The cord was tied to the chains of the corpse beside her. Kate sat up straight, forcing a smile as Lisa returned. She was carrying a tackle box by her side, one hand behind her back concealing something from Kate's sight. Lisa set the box down, careful to not reveal her secret. She stood grinning over Kate for a minute. Just when Kate didn't think she could bear the horrible suspense anymore, Lisa said, "Surprise!" She brought a dress from behind her back, using both hands to hold it in front of her so that Kate could see. "What do you think?" she asked excitedly.

Kate looked at the fancy yellow dress, complete with puffed sleeves and lace edging. It reminded her of something a doll would wear. She realized that was exactly what she would soon become. "It's gorgeous!" she exclaimed as soon as she could find her voice. "Do I get to wear that?"

"Uhuh," Lisa nodded. "After your makeover."

Dropping the dress in a crumpled pile, Lisa knelt next to the box, opening it. She rummaged around for a moment, and then withdrew a large pair of scissors, holding them high for Kate to see. For Kate, the scissors brought both fear and hope. They were large enough, sharp enough to kill. She had no idea how the girl next to her had died. On the other hand, they were also sturdy enough to free her of her bonds.

Lisa grabbed the rope around Kate's ankles and pulled, jerking her roughly away from the wall. "I always thought you'd look good with really short hair," she said as she knelt behind Kate. "Or maybe a bob. What do you think?"

Clearing her throat, Kate said, "I don't know Lisa. Which do you think would look better with the dress?"

"Hmmm. I think the bob. I have some ribbon we can use as a headband that will match. Now hold your head straight, you don't want a lopsided new do." She giggled at her own joke.

Kate listened to the sharp snap of the scissors. She fought tears as over a foot of hair length slid down her shoulder onto her lap. She willed herself pliant, her head bending whichever way Lisa pulled. Finally the snipping stopped. She heard the beautiful soft clink of the scissors being set on the ground behind her. Lisa rose and walked to face Kate and admire her handy work.

"Perfect," she said with an air of satisfaction. "Oh, but

you want to see too, don't you?" Lisa pulled the box to her and began rifling through the contents. Kate felt behind her for the scissors, her fingers stretching vainly as she searched everywhere within her reach. One finger managed to make contact, but the tool was too far away. She'd have to lean to get them within her grasp.

Lisa withdrew a mirror with a triumphant flourish. Kneeling over Kate's legs, she held the small compact open for Kate to see. Seizing the opportunity, Kate turned both directions, leaning from side to side as if she were inspecting the cut from every angle until the scissors were clenched tightly in her fist. Only then did she actually look in the mirror.

"Oh... wow," she said softly, a single tear escaping, sliding down her cheek as she saw the butchered mess atop her head. "You've made me so happy, Lisa. Thank you." The words slowly faltered out of her mouth.

Lisa grinned widely. "I knew you'd be a good playmate."

Kate manipulated the scissors in her hand, slowly trying to cut through her fetters undetected.

"Now the make-up."

Lisa turned her back as she searched in the tackle box. Kate used the opportunity to extend her range of motion as she sawed through the rope binding her wrists. She felt a slackening as the cord released its grip. She tucked the scissors under her butt, unsure when she'd get a chance to free her feet.

Lisa turned to face her, her hands full with tubes of paint and a brush. "Now some make-up," she said.

Kate's eyes widened as she saw what Lisa held. "Is that what you're going to use?"

Lisa nodded. "It works much better. Stays on much longer. I learned that with Gabby." She gestured towards the corpse.

"Lisa, that stuff is toxic."

Lisa looked at her blankly.

"It could kill me," Kate said.

"I thought you wanted to do this," Lisa whined, eyes narrowing. "I thought you were my friend. But you're not. You're just like the rest of them."

Shannon Hollinger

"Them? Lisa, how long have you been playing here?"

"Oh, years," she said casually. "I bring all my friends here eventually. But they all turn out to be nasty and ungrateful, like you."

"Lisa, I didn't mean to hurt your feelings. Honest. If you say that stuff works the best, then it has to be okay, right? You wouldn't do anything to hurt me. We're friends."

Lisa nodded enthusiastically, again smiling wide.

"Then let's get started."

Lisa set the oil paints up in a row beside Kate's thigh. She unscrewed the lid of each tube, setting them carefully aside. Then she crouched over Kate, balancing on her heels. She took Kate's face in her hand, turning it roughly. "Foundation first," she said. She reached beside her for a tube, and then froze. She made a choking noise, blood gurgling from her lips, staining them a bright crimson. She slowly turned and met Kate's eyes.

"I'm sorry," Kate cried, tears streaming down her face. She gave a violent jerk on the scissors, twisting them deeper inside Lisa's neck. Lisa reached for her, the hand dropping limply before it made contact. Kate shoved Lisa to the side, squirming across the dirt to distance herself a few feet before she struggled with the rope around her ankles. She came to a stop against the corpse. She could smell a musty odor rising off its surface, somewhere beneath layers of perfume.

Kate tugged at the knots, not wanting to have to retrieve the scissors. Feeling them loosen under her prying fingers, she continued to work at them until she was free. Jumping to her feet, she stared down at Lisa's crumpled form, a large halo of blood still growing around her head. Moving toward the mouth of the cave, she paused.

Kate battled with her curiosity. Then she turned, picked up a rack of candles, and slowly tiptoed toward whatever was in the dark at the back of the cavern. Holding her breath, she raised the light, illuminating the depths. She remained still for a moment, saying a silent prayer. She shed the light on each face in turn, giving each member of the lost their moment to be found. Then Kate turned her back on the semicircle of once-human dolls arranged along the back of the cave. The only thing she could do for them was live. Escape and live so that she could tell their loved ones where they could be found.

Turning to leave, an object on the floor beside her foot caught her eye. Kate squatted and set the candles down. Retrieving the tea cup from the ground, she cradled it in both of her hands. It had the same floral pattern as the set she had played with as a child. For a moment Kate was lost in thought, reminiscing about times long gone, of being a little girl, of tea parties and make-overs and a time in her life when things were just simpler. Easier. Happier. Kate scanned the cave, which really wasn't such a bad place. It was cool, and spacious, and now that her vision had adjusted, it wasn't even really that dark. Her eyes landed on the rest of the tea set, off to the side, sitting on a tray just like the one she had always wanted but her parents had never bought her. Kate looked at the tea set, neatly arranged and ready for a party, and smiled as she sat down to play with her new friends.

THE END

About the Author: With degrees in Crime Scene Technology and Physical Anthropology, Shannon Hollinger hasn't just seen the dark side of humanity – she's been elbow deep inside of it! She currently lives in New Hampshire where she is owned by two terriers and, when allowed, spends her free time writing and climbing mountains. To see where you can find more of her work, check out www.shannonhollinger.com.

Bert and Bones

John Kaniecki

"Thank you for calling Quickie Caskets, the casket our customers are just dying to get into." Kurt felt like a total idiot. But hey, he reasoned, times were hard and the threat of being homeless in January was a harsh reality. One he wanted to avoid at any cost, even if it meant taking a job as a customer service agent for a discount coffin dealer.

"Yes, do you have any oak caskets?" an anonymous voice over the phone asked.

Kurt's eyes scanned the papers overloaded with facts that were sitting on the desk before him. Frustrated, he pressed the mute button on the phone and called out to his colleague, Bell. "Do we have any oak caskets?"

The lovely lady blinked her long eye lashes and smiled sweetly. In a soft voice she answered, "We have the Stretcher line and the Comfort line."

Kurt was lost in a dream dazzled by the radiant beauty's charm. "Oh yes, and there's the Eleganza as well," she added. Kurt was somewhere in a fantasy, one starring a certain Bell. Drifting into his dream world he neglected his conversation with the caller, but reality came in the form of an angry squawking over the phone.

Kurt spent hours pondering some solution with only blanks filling his mind. He had lost count of the resumes he had sent out, though he was confident it was well over one hundred. Thank God for emails; the cost of snail mail postage would have severely cut into his meager funds. His diet these days consisted of cold franks and beans as that was all he could afford. This—and the fact that he was alone—drove him to the Salvation Army on Thanksgiving Day in search of a hot meal.

Apparently he wasn't the only one who felt that way, because the crowd there rivaled the bargain hunters who would be out looking for sales the next day. Kurt had to wait in line for over an hour for his plate. The turkey was dry and the green beans were awful, but the dressing and cranberry sauce were okay. Kurt was a bit frightened by the desperate crowd, but he was comforted by the fact that he wasn't alone in his woes.

He did his best to keep his spirits up, making a diligent effort to find work, clicking away daily on the computer and endlessly searching job sites. But as time progressed with no response except generic form letters, his mood grew dark and hopelessness set in. Why bother trying when all he would receive was a negative response addressed to 'Dear Applicant'?

Then one day the phone rang. The caller i.d. identified the caller as 'unknown'. Kurt was praying it was not a telemarketer or an annoying computer generated message when he picked up the phone and gave a hello. "Is this Kurt Baxter?" asked a man's deep voice.

"Yes, it is," Kurt said, hoping the man couldn't hear the desperation in his voice.

"I'm calling about the job you applied for," spoke the voice. Kurt could not believe what his ears were hearing.

Kurt stared at Bell. The woman was hard at work as usual and she was quite a sight. Bell was not his ideal image of beauty. She had short, thick, black hair that was spiked on top. Her eye shadow was a deep purple, with neatly plucked thin black eyebrows over them and she wore black lipstick. On her neck was a silver cross necklace and there was a skull and bones ring on one finger.

Kurt was usually attracted to the bubble headed, big breasted, blonde cheerleader type, but Bell was so far away from that. It was as if he had lived his entire life admiring roses only to chance upon a violet's beauty.

The phone rang on Kurt's desk, startling him from his lustful admiration. "Thank you for calling Quickie Caskets, the caskets our customers are just dying to get into," he said as he answered the phone.

A high, irritating squeaky voice spoke, "This is Bert Burtson, and I need a casket."

"Yes sir, Mister Burtson," said Kurt casually. "What kind of casket do you need?"

Bell's head jerked up, a look of torment on her face. "Oh my God is that Bert?" she asked in a barely audible guarded whisper.

Kurt was alarmed by Bell's reaction. Nervously he asked, "What kind of coffin do you need?"

"Same as usual," the squeaky voice replied.

Kurt let out a grand sigh as he parked his car in the parking lot of the funeral home for his job interview. Quickie Caskets was located across the street from a dilapidated cemetery. The fence around the cemetery grounds was rusted and broken with many gaping holes, and the grass had grown wildly out of control. The visible tombstones were vandalized with graffiti or smashed. Somewhere in Kurt's memories was the admonition not to disrespect the dead. Kurt felt a chill, not knowing if it came from the winter wind or the thought of the dead being disgraced.

As he stood staring at the building Kurt had a host of unanswered questions. *Why did they pick me? What do I have to do? How do I dress? Will I be working with the dead directly?* He tried to calm his nerves and appear confident. Despite his misgivings, he really needed this job. He dressed in all black as if he was attending a funeral; he thought that would be the most appropriate attire.

Kurt walked up the stone steps to the door. Two grim, stone gargoyles stood on either side of the door as if standing guard. Kurt pushed the doorbell with an extended finger quivering in fear. There was a loud gong, so loud it could perhaps wake the dead.

"That's burt Burtson?" Bell asked again. Her face was twisted in panic.

Kurt pressed the mute button so his voice could not be heard on the phone. "Yes it is," he stammered, Bell's panic being contagious. "Why, who is he?"

"Uh…nobody," Bell said, biting her lip and looking away.

"Come on, Bell," demanded Kurt. The young lady had never been anything but upfront and honest in the five weeks they had worked together.

"Hello, hello," cried the squeaky voice over the phone, "Is anybody there?"

"Well," said Bell, looking all around the room so as not to look at Kurt. "He's a…" She paused as her fingers nervously fidgeted. "He's an old…well actually." She gave a long deep sigh and finally confessed, "He's a very ancient boyfriend of mine."

Kurt pressed the mute button so his communications could be heard. "How can I help you, sir?" The young man spoke with bravado determined not to be bullied around. He was as a gallant knight defending his lady.

"I don't like the temper of your voice, boy," shot back the voice with a sound like a squeaky wheel.

Kurt got flustered. Customer service, he recalled, was all about making the client happy. This was his first call to be classified as 'escalated'.

The fear of being fired humbled his ego. "I'm sorry, sir," said Kurt meekly, glancing at Bell with a pitiful look. She had a vacant look on her face as she stared blankly past him.

"Do you know who this is?" the high, irritating voice was now screaming in rage.

"Yes, sir," said Kurt pathetically as he feared loosing his job. "You're Bert Burtson."

"That's right," said the annoying voice, "It's Bert Burtson. And I want the usual casket, in the usual way, at the usual place, tomorrow night."

"And where is that?" asked Kurt.

"517 Shade Maple Ave," there was a click and then a dial tone.

Kurt sat across from Mister Cloak, the owner of Quickie Coffins. He was dressed in a polite outfit resembling an usher's. The pin on his tie was a miniature skull and bones. "Despite the bad economy the casket business isn't dead." Mister Cloak's serious face gave a mischievous smile.

Kurt felt uncomfortable with the joke and didn't know how to react.

"You'll fit in good here," observed Mister Cloak, "you are rather stiff." The smiling face beamed into a broad grin.

Kurt looked down at the floor avoiding any eye contact.

"Don't worry," Mister Cloak assured, "we won't bury you with work." He let out a long chuckle.

Kurt sank deep into his chair.

"Just make sure you do a good job. We don't want to be haunted by our mistakes," concluded the business man as he extended his hand. "Congratulations. You're hired."

Despite the unsettling puns, Kurt eagerly shook Mister Cloak's hand. He didn't have a clue what the job description was, but he was too desperate to wonder.

Kurt had been assigned to personally deliver Bert Burtson's casket. He wanted to refuse, but Mister Cloak made it clear that his career as a customer service agent would come to an abrupt end if he didn't. Fear of rejoining the swelling ranks of the unemployed was the only thing that compelled him to oblige.

The casket had been loaded into the hearse already when Kurt arrived by its side. It was the first time he had driven this type of vehicle and sitting in the driver's seat was rather spooky. Everything about it filled Kurt with trepidation. His fingers stumbled over the buttons on the GPS unit in his sweaty palm. He was just starting to enter the address when he was startled by the passenger door opening.

Bell slid into the seat next to him, in Goth dress as usual. The only difference from her regular ensemble was she wore a hat which had a dark veil covering her face. She put her hand on Kurt's, wrapping her black nail polished fingers around them. "I don't want you to face Bert alone."

Unable to hide his mounting anger, Kurt snapped, "Aw, come on Bell. What the hell is going on here?"

Bell said nothing, only giving him a hurt and surprised look.

"Look, I'm sorry," Kurt confessed, "this is just bizarre."

Bell sat silent for a second before answering. "It's okay, sugar," she said reassuringly, squeezing his hand tight.

"Let's just do this" he said gruffly, blushing and hoping she couldn't see his sexual arousal from her touch.

Kurt placed the GPS on the hearse's leather dash board. "Turn left," said the computerized voice. Kurt turned the keys and the engine roared.

After driving only 200 yards the GPS proclaimed, "Your destination is on the right." Kurt was certain something was wrong. There was nowhere to turn except into the cemetery. Kurt squinted his eyes to read what was written on the arch above the drive. 'Burtson and Son's Cemetery, 517 Shade Maple Avenue.'

Kurt turned his head to Bell hoping for some explanation. Bell returned his gaze undaunted, "This is the place," she said calmly.

"Why are we delivering a casket to a cemetery in the dark? I was expecting a funeral home." Bell didn't answer, so he shrugged and drove into the cemetery. Kurt trusted his dark lady in silence.

The oversized vehicle bumped up and down on the gravelly road. There were no lights other than the car's headlights and a faint glow from the moon. They came to several places where the road split into two paths. At each intersection Bell pointed out the proper way. Finally, Bell whispered, "Stop here."

Kurt depressed the brake and the hearse came to an abrupt stop. "Thank God he's not here," Bell said. "Keep the car running. Let's unload quickly and get out of here," she continued as she opened to door to exit. "And above all, be quiet."

Kurt thought of the absolute absurdity of the situation. It was a cold January night. It was pitch black. He was inside a dilapidated cemetery delivering a coffin to some mysterious figure named Bert Burtson. How much stranger could things get?

"Come on," urged Bell as they tugged on the casket together. The casket rolled out smoothly. Kurt looked at it as it came out. The bottom was like a normal casket but the top was extremely wide, so wide that it was barely able to fit into the hearse.

Suddenly there was a cracking noise in the distance. Kurt looked at Bell in the dim light. "Oh my God! It's Bert!" she exclaimed.

Kurt looked up but saw nothing. He looked at Bell who met his glance. She looked relieved, maybe even excited.

"Great. Let's lower this down," Bell said in relief. The two grabbed a handle on each side of the casket and lowered it off the rails.

Suddenly the coffin lid popped open and banged into Kurt. The blow of the collision knocked him down to the ground as he fell on his back.

Out of the coffin emerged some hideous beast far from human. The green-colored monster had a gigantic head a half dozen times that of a human being. Its right eye was blood red, while its left was a blank socket. There was only a hint of a nose. As the creature gave a ferocious growl, it opened wide its large mouth exposing long sharp teeth. Kurt saw the massive size of the beast as it stepped out of the coffin. The young man was amazed as if he observed some magic trick. There was no way the monster could have fit inside the coffin. It was little comfort that the monster possessed only one arm, a claw-like appendage. The beast focused its good eye upon Kurt who was lying on the ground. The young man shook in fear as the beast licked its lips as if hungry.

"Oh Bert, baby," said Bell with admiration, "You're always full of surprises." The dark lady let off a long sigh of affection.

"Come on, honey," said Bert in a high whining voice, "it's dinner time."

THE END

About the Author: John Kaniecki resides in Montclair, New Jersey with his wife Sylvia of over eleven years. John volunteers as a missionary at the Church of Christ at Chancellor Avenue which is in the inner city of Newark, New Jersey. John is a writer and poet. He has two poetry books "Murmurings of a Mad Man" published by eLectio Publishing and "Poet to the Poor, Poems of Hope to the Bottom One Percent" by Dreaming Big Publications. In addition he has a science fiction collection entitled "Words of the Future" published by Witty Bard and a horror novella "Scarecrow, Scarecrow" published by Fat-Lip Press.

His Own Eyes

Ray Dean

Sandwich Islands, 1886

There were few things that could interrupt Caleb Glenn's supper, and the appearance of one of his employees at the door wasn't one of them. His wife showed the man around back to the kitchen door and quietly offered to bring him a chair to join them in their meal, but the man wisely refused. Standing on the step just outside the screened door, Tucker bent the brim of his hat under his grasping fingers and waited for Caleb to acknowledge him.

A small chop was duly cut and half consumed as the plantation owner managed to ignore the lean man standing stock still in the shade of a lilikoi vine. But he could not avoid the look of censure from his wife as she refused his open-handed request for the platter of meat. She tilted her head toward the door and waited for him to reply.

Pushing his fork into his greens, Caleb pried open his clenched jaw and demanded, "You were in the eastern fields this morning... what does it look like?"

Tucker shifted from one foot to the other, rubbing the worn leather uppers of his boots together. "Cane's over twice the size of the workers, Boss. We've got a week before the plants start to flower."

Swallowing what was in his mouth, Caleb answered back. "Then we'd best set to burnin' in the next day or two. Need to get ahead instead of just tryin' to beat the flowers, especially in this heat."

Tucker waved off the silent offer of coffee from Mrs. Glenn. "That might be a problem, Boss."

Caleb's fork clattered onto the plate. "And why is that?"

"The men... well, they're all planning to leave." His voice barely squeezed out of his throat. "Every one of them Japanese workers is leaving with their families as soon as they can pack up their wagons."

Scraping back his chair, Caleb left his napkin lying in the middle of his half-finished supper. "The hell they are."

Tucker preceded him into the yard and handed him the reins of the extra horse he'd brought with him, but neither man acknowledged the tremulous shake in Tucker's cold fingers. They swung up into the saddle and Caleb followed Tucker into the unaccustomed darkness.

"Why is this the first I'm hearing of this?"

"Work was lagging today, the men and women were tired." Adjusting the gait of his horse he pulled closer to Caleb's mount. "One of the women said the workers' village was haunted."

A bitter curse spat from his lips. "Superstition is no excuse, Tucker."

"That's what I said, Boss," he turned his head slightly down and away, his eyes firmly on his hands as they clutched the reins. "But they seemed... scared. Really scared."

"I want to talk to that woman. I want to hear it for myself and then we'll get the workers back doing what they need to do. I'm not going to waste any time on this, hup!" Kicking his horse into a faster gait, Caleb pulled ahead even as he barked out more questions with only a slight turn of his head. He was only half aware that Tucker was answering him and understood even less of the wind-torn words.

Caleb had worked plantations in Louisiana and stretched his skills in Haiti for a few seasons. He had no problem managing people. He took fields and made them profitable.

He took legions of men and turned them into a workforce. He didn't have time for fear and superstition. The kinds of people that believed in superstition, spirits, and curses were the kind of backwards, small-minded people that were perfect for hard labor. He just had to set them straight. He'd explain away this 'haunting' and then they'd get back to the matter at hand. They had sugarcane to harvest.

Where his own house was situated on a rise with a view of the fields and a blue swath of ocean down past the point, the workers' village, even in the long afternoon shadows of dusk, looked as if it had been carved from the lush sugarcane fields that they tended. Originally, the small square homes had been at the edge of the Consolidated Union Sugar Company's holdings, but a neighboring cotton plantation had gone out of business and Comstock Union himself had purchased the land for pennies on the dollar. Leaving the workers' homes where they were, they merely added more sugar cane were they could, fairly hemming in the little cottages.

As they drew up closer, Tucker pointed out a cottage on the edge of the village, its steps were pieced together from the abundant stores of volcanic rock that they'd dug out of the ground before they'd planted. Tucker eased up on the reins a bit, loosening the choke hold he'd had on them since they'd begun their ride. He stopped and hobbled his horse near a patch of weeds and took Caleb's reins and did the same as his boss worked out the stiffness in his leg.

Snatching his hat from his head and slapping the dust across his pant leg, Caleb followed Tucker to the cottage and up onto the landing outside the front door. Tucker removed his hat as well and pounded on the door frame, making the screened frame bounce with its force.

A young boy pushed open the door and stood with his back to it, holding it open. His blunt cut bangs fell back from his tanned forehead as he looked at the strangers. He watched the two men walk in with their heavy boots, dirt chunking off onto the straw mats covering the floor, and ran off into a back room.

Seated on the floor, two women who bore some familial resemblance to each other sat quietly with their legs tucked under themselves as was their custom. Tucker gestured at Caleb and spoke to the woman in a mix of languages that made Caleb's head hurt.

She answered him with a nod and gestured to the younger woman. "My niece, Kumiko," she explained, "told me that she saw Shizuko in the village."

"Why doesn't she tell us?" Caleb wasn't a man that liked to wait for what he wanted.

Tucker was the one who answered. "The girl came by boat a few months ago, boss. She hardly speaks a word other than Japanese and what she knows is more *pidgin* than anything." When Caleb didn't say anything, Tucker gestured to the younger woman. "Tell us."

The young woman fairly cowered before them, her work-roughened hands tucked demurely in her lap as she rattled off words in her native language, there were English words in there as Tucker had predicted, but they were difficult to understand and peppered with odd words that seemed a mix of tongues. The older woman sitting beside her on the matted floor kept her eyes on Caleb and when the girl stopped speaking, her aunt explained. "Kumiko said that the woman is '*ubumei*.'"

Caleb's expression darkened with distrust. "I thought you said the woman was Shizuko."

The older woman's eyes flashed him a look. "Her name was Shizuko, but now she is *ubumei*..." her expression was inwardly thoughtful as though she were trying to find the right way to explain, "a lost mother spirit." Her expression softened as she lifted her hands, pressing them against her dark kimono's rounded bosom. "Her soul longs for her child." She looked up at them and it seemed to Caleb, when the lantern flickered in a sudden breeze, that there was a shimmer of tears in the corner of her eye. "Shizuoka never held her child. Never heard her child cry. She longs for the child she left behind."

Tucker huffed out a breath. "Superstition! Are you making up stories?"

Her dark gaze avoided his. "A mother worries for her child for all time. There is no lie in that."

Both of the men heard the weighty sorrow in her tone and neither of them wanted to delve further into the topic. Instead Caleb turned his thoughts to the more immediate matter. "You can't believe this… this ghost story!" Turning on his heel, Caleb headed for the horses.

Tucker caught up to him halfway. "Maybe we should listen to the old woman, Boss." He put a hand on Caleb's shoulder to stop him and started when Caleb shrugged it off. "Everyone in the village listens to her."

"The more we talk to her, the more they think she knows what she's talking about." Nodding at the street, they saw curious eyes darting their way. The workers were curious and watching them intently. Lowering his voice and sparing a look for the little village and any curious onlookers in the lengthening shadows, Caleb shook his head. "Just because she knows some fancy words about ghosts and other mumbo jumbo, doesn't mean I have to waste more of my time on her ridiculous story."

"But they're leaving!" Tucker stepped to the side and pointed at the wagons loaded with boxes of goods and rough-hewn sacks.

"Damn superstitious idiots!" Caleb stalked across the clearing and grabbed at the shoulder of one of the men, nearly knocking something from his arms. "Put that back in the house." When the man didn't move he turned to face men on the other side of the wagon struggling to lash a wooden chair to the back. "You, there, put these things back. Now!"

They stared at him, eyes barely blinking and limbs tense with fear.

Caleb reached for the pouch on his belt and pulled his

knife free. With a well-placed slash, two ropes were loosed and fell back into the shadows. With his free hand, Caleb grabbed a stool from the top of the pile and crossed to the closest home. With a pointed look at the quickly assembling crowd he tossed the stool onto the lanai and barely kept himself from cringing as the heavy bounce of the wood echoed off of the walls.

"Boss, wait."

Stepping away from Tucker, Caleb climbed a step of the home and peered into the shadowed faces, waiting for someone to challenge him. "Well?" He swept his gaze over the rapidly assembling group. "Is that why you're leaving? Some old woman's fanciful story?"

They didn't answer him, not in words. He saw the fear etched deeply in the lines of their faces, darkened by long shadows in the twilight, until they were as deep as the irrigation ditches that cut through the plantation's fields. In their eyes he saw the truth. They were frightened... for their very lives.

"*Ai ya!*" A woman's frightened shout sent a chill through Caleb even though he refused to acknowledge it with more than a furtive shake of his head. Her voice cut through his haze a second time. "*Obake!*"

He turned, following her trembling hand as she pointed toward the cane field on the other side of the irrigation ditch. A wisp of color danced through the cane leaves, trailing cold light even under the rising harvest moon. It outlined each razor-sharp spine as it passed, flared bright behind the spindly legs of a cane spider strung between blades, and at the edge of the field it spun with anxious energy, moving forward and backward as if it was pacing the ground.

Everyone was silent, the only sound was the driving water in the irrigation ditch between them and the light. And the light was moving, leaving the relative cover of the sugarcane and drawing closer to the muddy slope down to the *auwai*.

Some of the doors behind him slammed shut on fearful voices, but others were thrown open by curious villagers running to join the rest outside. Some of them held their belongings in their hands, caught in the process of packing. They let them tumble from their hands into the dirt as a figure broke free of the undulating shadows of the sugarcane leaves.

Voices rose up from the villagers. They called for Hitoshi to come to protect them. Their words, the very fear that blanched their complexions, brought the young man to the door. Once considered ruggedly handsome, his loss had ripped away much of his youth and vitality away from him. His worn hands clutched his swaddled child haphazardly to his chest as he struggled to peer across the clearing toward the cane. His eyes followed the frantic gestures of pointed fingers to the slight form wrapped in a white kimono hovering on the far bank of the *auwai*.

The infant, struggling against his rough embrace let loose with a fearful howl and suddenly everyone around them grew still.

The hollow splash of water against the banks of the auwai echoed from the thin wooden walls of the plantation houses. Plodding a ponderous rhythm through the darkness, each hollow splosh of noise rattled up Caleb's spine and he made a conscious effort to stand tall in the darkness even though no one was looking in his direction.

All eyes followed Hitoshi as he made his way toward the ditch. His child, lungs raging, squirmed in his hands. Hitoshi had no control of the boisterous child when his own attention was fixed before him. Shizuko, her dark hair tumbled down around her shoulders, bore little resemblance to the winsome young woman she had been when they'd married. The kimono hung over her body like laundry on the line, as if what lay beneath the moonlit garment was merely bone instead of body.

The steps continued through the water, climbing up on the earthen bank, and pushed those gathered further back with fear alone. They had seen the face before. They had all known her in life, but what gathered their fear around them like a heavy shroud was that her figure seemed to hover above the ground, her legs lost to the shadows of night. The thick sucking sound of mud and deepening footholds in the ground gave weight to the floating shape.

Caleb scarcely felt the ground beneath his own feet as his half-eaten supper tumbled in his gut. He felt Tucker trembling beside him, heard the young man's swift intake of breath and then the muttered curse a heartbeat later.

Hitoshi was transfixed. He moved not. He spoke not. His face, hidden from Caleb's view, was turned up toward the hovering spectre advancing toward him.

"Her hands," Tucker's voice was hoarse under the whispered tone, "look at her hands."

One of the blue lights darted around her middle and Caleb saw her hands. Hanging from her wrists as if they no longer held bone, her hands seemed to undulate with the plodding movement of her form. She closed the distance and her image moved down, dropping closer to the ground as though she had found a way to kneel on invisible legs.

"The baby," again it was Tucker's voice drawing his attention, the younger man's fear bleeding into his own mind, "don't let her touch the baby!"

Hitoshi made no move. He barely held the infant in his hands as the child struggled against him.

Caleb felt his own emotions warring with his mind. He cared little for these people, he barely knew their pay numbers let alone their names, but he was still a man, and a God-fearing man at that. Setting aside his fear he began to move, a step and then another.

The hand on his arm was strong, vicelike. When he turned to argue with Tucker he met the eyes of the old woman. She shook her head. "Stay." The word sounded foreign on her tongue but the meaning in her eyes was clear.

Caleb looked back and the only thing stronger than his fear for the child was the woman's grip on his arm.

The ghost, if indeed that was what she was, hovered over her child, her face turning this way and that as she studied the bundle that seemed to sprout arms and legs from his swaddling.

A hiccup of sound, something akin to a laugh, floated on the air, shattered the heavy fear that had settled over them. The child reached up his hands toward the glow of light above him.

And his mother, a new expression twisting her features, reached out to touch her living child, and failed. Her hands were useless, impotent.

The voice that ripped through his ears was full of rage and desperation. Sorrow, thick and heartbreaking, weighed on his shoulders and he knew with certainty that it was not his own emotions rolling him under with their power.

Hitoshi shook his head back and forth, words spilled from his lips begging with their tone, yet the woman's screams continued on as she backed away, almost slithering down the muddy bank and slipping into the dark rushing water.

His ears ringing with noise, it took Caleb a few minutes to realize that the cries flooding him with sound came from the baby clutched in Hitoshi's arms. He could not console the infant, nor could he stop his own mournful cries.

"What happened?" Caleb turned to the old woman who still held his arm tight. "What happened to that woman?"

"The water," she began, her voice moaning with sorrow, "Shizuko fell into the water."

Tucker had moved closer, nodding at the woman's words, verifying the truth.

"She gave birth to baby, but family need money, so she went back to fields to work beside husband. Beside Hitoshi-san. Sun too hot. Work too hard."

Caleb knew the layers of clothing that all the workers wore around the cane. Thick layers of cloth wrapped around their limbs to protect their skin from the razor-sharp leaves, clothing lashed tightly to their bodies to keep out the vicious bite of the cane spider when it crept up their limbs, and the stinging bite of the centipedes as they struggled to slip under and feel the warmth of living flesh. On a hot day, the workers fairly boiled in their own clothing.

"Shizuko," she sighed, "went to the *auwai* to drink the

water. She leaned too far, fell in. No one could reach." She looked up into Caleb's face, her skin streaked with tears. He knew what it was like. The irrigation ditches had planks laid across the water for people to cross the swiftly moving stream. A soft gasp drew his attention again.

"*Reikon,* her spirit, no can rest. No peace until we make funeral for her body."

Tucker nodded, his eyes fixed in the dark shadows around their feet. "We followed the ditch for miles, searching the brush, hoping to find her."

"The ditch," spat the old woman, "goes to the sea. We find nothing. No body to bring home to Hitoshi. No body to bring home to baby."

"The body," Caleb felt the evening chill on his skin, "without the body..."

"Her spirit," she continued to speak even as her body trembled, "will remain."

"Why," Caleb turned on the other man. "Why didn't you tell me about this?"

Tucker's eyes snapped cold. "You said you didn't want to know the problems, Boss. You said you only wanted to know the work we had done."

Caleb was shamed by the truth in Tucker's words. He had given Tucker those very instructions and turned a blind eye everything else. "Tomorrow," he promised them, "tomorrow we begin to search again."

He turned to the old woman and met her curious gaze. "Tell them to stay. Tell them we will find her body." Hitoshi passed by, villagers supporting him on both sides as they led him toward his home, another struggling to calm the sobbing infant. "Tell them... ask them for their help." Caleb didn't see the old woman leave; his focus was the dark irrigation ditch a short distance away. He couldn't explain the strange push he felt within as he began to move in search of his horse. He knew he would not be able to explain any of this to his wife when he returned home. He doubted that he would ever be able to explain what he'd seen to anyone, even though he'd seen it with his own eyes.

THE END

About the Author: Living History and Reenacting has got to mess with your head... at least a little. Right? At least that's what Ray Dean keeps telling her friends and family. All that time spent in another time has a lasting effect in how you look at the world. Add in a little of the creative magic of theater and you might understand why creating characters and stories is such a rush. Historical settings are her first love, but there is something heady about twisting the threads of time into little knots and creating new timelines to explore. There are endless possibilities that she is just beginning to discover.

Ray Dean was born and raised in Hawaii where she spent many a quiet hour reading and writing stories. Performing in theater and working backstage lead her into the delights of Living History, creating her own worlds through writing seemed the next logical step. Historical settings are her first love, but there is something heady about twisting the threads of time into little knots and creating new timelines to explore. There are endless possibilities that she is just beginning to discover.

Website: My Ethereality www.raydean.net
email: raydean219@gmail.com
facebook: https://www.facebook.com/RayDeanAuthor
Amazon Author page: http://www.amazon.com/Ray-Dean/e/B009ZZE8B8

....AND LOSE HIS OWN SOUL

JOHN ROBINSON

It was a cold November afternoon, the sky grey and heavy with clouds. The park was practically abandoned except for the black car sitting idle in the empty parking lot.

Officer Jim Hult drove his cruiser into the parking lot. The only other car in the lot was the black one, just as Dispatch had informed him. Hult whistled as he parked slightly behind the 1976 limited edition Ford Gran Torino. A call had come in, from a concerned jogger or senior citizen out for a walk Hult assumed, fearful of something unsavory. The car had been there for a while and had obviously made someone skittish.

Hult radioed Dispatch and got out. He approached the idling car cautiously. Through the window he could see a man inside, slumped in the driver's seat, sleeping. He rapped a knuckle on the window, then again, harder, when the man didn't stir. Hult slapped the car roof until the man jerked awake.

Chris looked up at the policeman staring down at him through the window. The car was so warm, and, he had to admit, the seat so presently comfortable, he wished he could ignore the law enforcement officer. He sat up, body aching, that familiar pain that was, lately, all too constant in his stomach. He wondered how long he had been out.

Chris rolled the window down. "Yes, officer?" He wiped sleep from his eyes, vision clearing, focusing.

"Good evening, sir," the policeman said. "Driver's license, please."

Chris pulled his wallet from his coat pocket, handed over his license.

The officer looked it over. "Mr. Linney. What are you doing sleeping in your car, sir?"

Chris tried to shake a fuzziness from his head. "I was on my way home, officer, and I got sleepy."

"You got sleepy?"

"Yes, sir," Chris said. "I'm on medication. One of them is new. I guess I haven't got used to it yet."

"What medication is that, Mr. Linney?" the officer asked.

Chris reached to the passenger seat and held up a gallon freezer bag of prescription pill bottles.

"May I see those, Mr. Linney?"

"Sure," Chris handed them over.

"Give me a minute," Hult said and walked back to the cruiser, inspecting the pill bottles through the plastic.

Chris leaned back in his seat. His head had begun to swim a little, the world rotating slowly around him. Circling, see-sawing. He felt the urge to vomit, but that quickly passed when a cold but refreshing breeze burst through the window and froze his face.

He looked at his watch. "Almost an hour," he muttered. The nap had been good, though, if now slightly troublesome.

In the rearview mirror, he could see the police officer in his car, cell phone to his ear. He was watching Chris, nodding to something said on the other end. The officer's expression had changed, softened from the hard professional glare it was before. Chris recognized that look the policeman was wearing. Sympathy. Pity.

Officer Hult walked back to Chris's car and handed the bag of meds and his driver's license back to him. "Mr. Linney, if you are unable to drive, you should get someone to drive for you. It is dangerous driving while impaired, not just for you but for others too."

"I know, officer. I thought I was okay," Chris said, "but it just kind of came over me all of a sudden. That's why I stopped here at the park."

"I understand," Officer Hult said. "A passerby reported you sitting here, just making sure everything was on the up and up," he smiled uncomfortably.

"I'm sorry."

"It's okay, I guess." Hult shifted on his feet, hands on his hips. "I'm going to let you off with a warning, this time. Are you okay to drive? If not, I can take you home, or you can call someone to pick you up."

"I'm good now," Chris said. "I feel much better. I'm okay to drive."

"Okay, Mr. Linney. I can follow you home if you like," Hult offered.

"I'm okay, I don't live too far away," Chris said.

"You have a good evening, then," Officer Hult said. Before he turned away, he added: "I spoke with the pharmacy. They told me what kind of medicine....I'm sorry, Mr. Linney."

"Thank you," Chris said. He stared ahead of him, at the row of trees that bordered the park from the neighborhood beyond. He stared at the houses on the other side of those trees. He stared at one in particular.

The microwave beeped and Chris removed the plate of leftovers from the meal his sister had brought him three days earlier, on Sunday. Meatloaf, mashed potatoes, mac & cheese. He sat down at the table, fork in hand. It smelled wonderful, mouthwatering, but he just had no appetite. He sipped at his apple juice, which was all he found that tasted the way it should anymore.

He poked at the meatloaf, then ran the fork through the potatoes. He put a small bite of meat with a little mashed potato in his mouth, chewed, then swallowed. If asked, he wouldn't be able to really describe the taste. He wasn't sure if it was one pill or a combination of little wonders he had to thank for destroying his taste buds and appetite. Taste was a memory now—the rich flavors of history had ceded to the nothings of the present.

Chris scraped the food off the plate into the garbage can. He washed the plate, fork, and after drinking all the juice, dried them, then put them away in their proper places. In his room he sat down on the bed, the bag of meds on the nightstand. He opened his pill organizer and emptied the evening dose into his hand, and forced them down with bottled water.

He'd have to go to the doctor tomorrow after skipping out on his appointment today. He thought it was ironic that he didn't go to the doctor today because he hadn't felt well. Chris had driven halfway to his physician's office before being overcome with such a wave of nausea and drowsiness. He turned the car around and headed for the house; he saw the park and decided to stop. Good thing, in hindsight. The nap was nice, and even though it wasn't yet seven o'clock, fatigue had claimed him and he was ready to call it a day.

He dreaded what tomorrow would bring with it, other than the doctor visit. Every day now brought some new malfunction in his body. In the bathroom mirror, Chris noticed he had lost a little more weight. His shirt hung looser; not much, but enough for him to notice. His face looked thinner. He didn't quite look like a kid in an adult's clothes, but it wouldn't be long.

But he wouldn't look like a kid, would he? He wouldn't look like a young man, not at all. He already looked old, advanced beyond his years. Wrinkles were developing despite his skin looking tighter to his skull and already the color of ash.

Chris fell down at the toilet and puked. He opened his mouth and out it came, like squeezing the last bit of toothpaste from the tube. His body tensed, throat convulsed.

He slumped to the floor. A trembling hand reached up and pulled the lever. The bloody water was drained away.

I'll have to tell the doctor, Chris thought just before he passed out.

Chris sat on a rolling stool, back against the wall. Upton Bruer, or Uppty as Chris called him in their school days together, sat on the examination table.

"Then what?" Uppty asked.

"What? After I puked blood? I passed out on the floor," Chris said.

Uppty slung his stethoscope around his neck and ran his hands down the front of his white lab coat. "I don't think it's all the medication."

"I didn't think it was, either," Chris said.

"This is to be expected, though, Chris. I can prescribe something for nausea."

"No," Chris said. "I basically just take the pain pills anyway. I don't want anything else."

Uppty stared at him thoughtfully. There was a pleading rage building behind his eyes. "There's always treatment, you know. More extensive treatment."

"I know," said Chris, "and it may buy me a couple of months, but this is how I want it."

The doctor's jaw clenched.

Chris said, "You can only delay the inevitable for so long, Uppty."

"Chris-"

Chris snapped, "*Doctor* Bruer."

Uppty jumped down from the examination table. "I'm your doctor," he huffed.

"What do you advise as my friend?"

"I think you need a lot of help, Chris. That's my opinion as your personal physician, and as your friend."

Chris swiveled away from him.

"Do you still have it?" Uppty asked. "And don't play stupid."

Chris smiled briefly at him. "I have a lot of things, Uppty."

Uppty crossed his arms. "When you were first diagnosed,

and I mentioned treatment-"

"You have nothing to worry about, " Chris sighed.

"Were you serious?"

"No."

"Be honest, Chris," Uppty said. "We've known each other a long time, and I never thought you could, but…but I don't know about now. You said your .38 special was the only treatment you needed. Were you serious?"

"Uppty," Chris met his friend's gaze as best, as honest, as he could. "I didn't mean it."

"I don't think I completely believe you."

"You can rest easy," Chris said.

"You've made that too difficult already," Uppty said.

"I don't expect you, or anybody, to support my decisions," Chris said. "I know you think this is my out."

"You're a conceited bastard, you know that?" Uppty said. "You don't want to live, but at least you can make dying a little easier on yourself."

"Easier on you." Chris cleared his throat. "Will you stop calling my sister and telling her my private information? I know it's you. Isn't that illegal?" He smiled, trying to diffuse the tension that had filled the suddenly very suffocating room.

"We all miss Penelope," Uppty said, ignoring Chris. "I know it's not easy losing your wife. Just remember we're losing you, too, now. We will have lost both of you."

Chris shook his head. He didn't want to cry, but felt tears coming anyway, felt his face flush. "Yeah, I know," he strangled on the words. "But I didn't lose her," he said walking out the door, "she was taken."

The sun broke free and the clouds dissipated to paint a smooth blue sky. The day became what the meteorologists on the evening newscasts would inevitably deem "unseasonably warm". The beauty that had become Thursday saw the park busy with joggers and stay at home parents pushing strollers, chatting, and keeping watchful eyes on toddlers and preschoolers while other people walked and talked and debated.

Chris's head began to swim as soon as he stood from the car. He breathed a minute. A bench was just right there, just a few feet away. He could make it; he had faith. The world tilted, rising and falling like waves on the ocean. Chris slid onto the hood of his car, reclined against the windscreen. The sun was warm on his face.

It hurt to lay there, but when did he not hurt? Everything was uncomfortable these days, everything was painful. Living was constant agony. He had his own idea of pain management. He knew it wasn't for everyone, he knew his family and friends were worried, angry, and sad. He knew they loved him, but hated him for the decisions he had made.

You're just torturing yourself, his sister, Judy, had told him. Maybe he was. Maybe he would regret everything in the final moments. Sometimes he regretted some of it already; he wouldn't have long to live with regrets, though.

The dizziness passed. There was a lightness still clogging his head when he moved, but that was something he had learned to live with. Painkillers equaled little to no pain, but they also equaled a high. He felt the fuzzies, medicine head. The world was in slow-mo, his mind and body in no gravity.

He sat up, rubbed his stomach. His bowels gurgled. He watched two little kids, a boy and a girl, run around the slides, kicking up sand. He listened to them laugh, their delighted squeals when they bumped into each other. It made Chris smile. He and Penelope had planned to have a child, possibly two, maybe three. They had talked about it often.

Chris zipped up his jacket and stood on stronger legs. Determination was fueling him, and he felt nearly invincible, even with an Achilles heel of a killer spreading throughout his body. Aches and pains be damned!

How many times had he and his wife visited this park? They had spent many wonderful days here. They walked and ran here, preparing for different marathons, played basketball and tennis with their friends. It was here that Chris first knew he wanted to spend the rest of his life with Penelope. It was here, in this park, on a beautiful, sunny, almost perfect day, that he knew he would ask her to be his wife. That day felt so distant to him, like a lot of things, as if it was a hundred years ago.

And funny to think, the instrument of his wife's death had been so close the entire time.

He reached into the car and weighed the gun in his hand. It felt heavier than it ever had. He put it in his coat pocket, hand resting on it, and slammed the car door.

Chris walked across the playground at a leisurely pace. He couldn't really hurry if he wanted to, despite how hard determination was firing his pistons. Foggy head, weak limbs— slow and steady would win the race.

The kids were laughing, screaming with joy as they slid down the tall slide. Their mother was clapping, cheering them on. Chris smiled as he passed them, but they didn't notice him. No one did, none of the other children or adults paid him any heed. Didn't notice, or chose not to see him. Either way it didn't matter.

He crossed the playground, and at the edge of the park where the trees stood sentry and kept the park from the residential area, he marched on. He looked up at the house before him; a nice place, affluent but not too flashy. He knew that the big back yard contained a, two-car garage, in-ground pool, and barbecue pit. Firmly upper middle class.

There was warm saliva flooding his mouth and he spat. His tongue felt thick, hairy. He bent over, mouth opened and let the spit fall freely. He had the urge to wretch, but swallowed it back and shrugged off the icy perspiration that broke out like a rash.

Chris picked up a decorative stone from the flower bed. Turning it over he saw the latch of the secret compartment and opened it. Inside was a key. He took the key and tossed the hideaway stone. He let himself in the back door, thankful there was no security system; he knew a lot, but not an alarm code.

The house hummed like all homes do in private. The refrigerator whirred, the fish tank bubbled, a board settled here, a clock ticked there. The kitchen let into the dining area and Chris sat down. The walk had exhausted him. The excitement tired him, the anticipation drained him. He was trembling. His scalp itched. Frosty beads of sweat dripped down his face.

He eased the gun from his pocket and rested it on the table, clutched in his grip. His knuckles were white. The nausea rose. A blackness crept across his vision. Chris stumbled to the kitchen and heaved into the sink, surprised to see blood rather than vomit spew from his mouth and splatter into the sink. His knees buckled and he collapsed on the floor, gun still in his hand.

When he couldn't lift his head, he gave up and closed his eyes.

As he lay on the kitchen floor, half conscious, his thoughts flashed back to the moment that changed his life forever. Unlike happier days, that night, the night he lost her, the night she was taken, didn't seem long ago, but current and immediate. He had woken up cold, bleeding, and shivering. He hurt all over. The taste of dirt was in his mouth, the smell of exhaust in his nose. There was a red light beside his face. His eyes were blurry and teary and it was dark, so very dark. He tried to reach for the light, whatever it was, but his arm didn't want to move at first. He had to wriggle his fingers, to let feeling come back one pin prick at a time.

Finally, his arm moved. The traffic baton.

"Penelope?" he moaned.

It came back to him slowly. The relay, the marathon. They were helping at the checkpoint. It was over with, time to pack up and go home.

"Penelope?" he called, louder.

They were walking up the road to the checkpoint, to the middle school parking lot. A truck had come. It was foggy.

It swerved-

"God, oh God," Chris crawled from the ditch.

-it swerved, crossed the highway, over the line, and he had tried to pull Penelope out of the way, he had her hand in his-

"Penelope!"

Frantic voices were running to them, blue lights quickly advancing.

-the truck had hit Penelope and pulled her from his grasp, tossing him aside.

The truck was nose-down in the ditch, taillights flashing.

Penelope was sprawled on the pavement. Chris crawled to her on his hands and knees, through her blood. Her arms were splayed at an odd angle, one leg bent back, her neck twisted-

"Oh, God!" He touched her cheek. He wanted to pick her up, to hold her, but drew his arms back. "Oh God!" he cried.

Chris tried to stand; his ankle snapped and he fell.

"You bastard," he crawled for the truck, dragging his leg.

"—an ambulance now!" Voices and lights were everywhere.

"Bastard!" he screamed. Hands were on him, holding him down. Voices were telling him to stay still, to remain calm. Someone was crying. Someone else was getting sick.

A man in a reflector vest was looking in the truck. "He's alive!"

Chris fought against the helping hands and clawed the pavement, screaming, crying, and yelling until his throat was sore and his voice hoarse.

Later on that fateful day, in the hospital, his sister Judy sat at his bedside. Her arms were crossed; she looked tired, worn out from worry. Her eyes red and puffy.

"Sis," Chris mumbled. He felt paralyzed, the world completely out of focus and his body nonresponsive. His arm flopped like a fish, IV in the back of his hand. He knew he had been drugged, even before the ambulance on the accident scene had left for the emergency room, they had stuck a needle in his arm and shot him up with something.

"Don't move, Chris," Judy told him and placed his hand on the bed.

"Penelope," he said. His mouth was dry, and he thought his tongue was cracking open. "Where is Penelope?" He was in a private hospital room, not an ER exam station. "Where is she?"

"Try to rest a little," Judy said.

"She's hurt," Chris said through tears. "She was hurt, Judy."

Judy stroked his hair. "I know." She wiped away tears, hers and his. "I know she was."

Chris moaned. "No," he said. "No, she's okay, she's gonna be okay…"

Judy patted his hand and sobbed silently. "Chris, I'm sorry."

Walter Green.

Chris had come to the conclusion that grief was mathematical. It added up. Penelope was gone. That was the worst possible event that could happen to him. The funeral arrangements had multiplied the pain. Visiting the funeral home, making the choices…it was piling up.

Deciding on a coffin (navy with white interior) plus the casket cover plus her dress (the blue one she wore every anniversary- a total of five for them) plus purchasing plots at the cemetery (two; one for her and a place for him, eventually, side by side) all equaled torment and hollowness. He was a shell, and he believed he was all cried out until the actual funeral, and then he not only cried some more, but Chris cried harder than he ever had before in his life. He broke down, he collapsed, he wailed. He was alone, empty of life. He was alone.

He was alone now, in house, shut off from the world, looking at the flowers that had been delivered. A simple message was written on the accompanying card:

"We are praying for you. Our sympathies, Walter and Debby Green."

Chris knew the name. Walter Green. He had first heard it muttered while he was still laid up in a hospital bed. Judy had told him. Walter Green. An elderly man, about seventy, and a heart patient. A "heart attack survivor" were Judy's words. He had suffered a massive heart attack behind the wheel-- he was the man driving the truck that ended Chris's world. It was an accident, just one of those chance things that happened and this time it happened to Chris and Penelope. Penelope was dead and Walter Green was a free man.

"He's lucky to be alive." Judy's words again. Lucky to be alive. "Just like you," she had added. But not Penelope, Chris had thought.

"Walter Green." Chris repeated the name each time he read the card, and he read it over and over. He tossed the flowers in the trash, found a box of matches and watched the card burn.

"Walter Green." The more times he said it, the more it stung.

It was as simple as looking in the telephone directory. There were several Greens listed, but, miracle of miracles, only one listing for, thank the heavens, Walter and Debby Green. Walter and Debby. No mistake. 1626 Matthew Street.

Chris found himself in the car. It had begun to snow, small flakes swirling and blowing, dusting the trees. It was beautiful, and he drove around town just looking at how nature was painted. He didn't consciously seek out the Green residence until he looked up and saw the street sign. Then it was a matter of turning the steering wheel and coasting down the lane.

GREEN was stenciled on the mailbox. The truck was in the drive. Lights were on.

Chris drove by, and turned. He pulled into the park, and, just as inexplicably as finding Matthew Street, found himself standing in the falling snow on the playground. The trees were bare to the bark and he could see through them to the houses on the other side.

He could see the rear of the Green home.

He found himself coming to the park more often. Before work. After work. His days off. He strolled the playground and the trails, the house always in his sight. He saw the Greens come and go, saw how Mr. Walter Green had recovered from his bad ticker, the progress he made. Chris watched them living their lives together as husband and wife. Leaning on each other for support. Walter had Debby, Debby had Walter. Who did Chris have?

A knot developed in Chris's stomach. Each day he came to the park and watched the house, the knot tightened. It was a sore that festered and eventually infected his entire body and being.

He didn't know when the thought first took root—maybe it had always been there. But the thought consumed him, and, if he were to confess it, that dark passion, its boiling persistence, is probably what promised to take his own life.

"It's cancer, Chris," Uppty had told him after all the tests were done. "It's..." and Uppty had not been able to finish, but Chris filled in the blanks. Fast, spreading, and terminal. Cancer, according to Uppty, was what was wrong, why the results of his blood work were abnormal, why he couldn't keep food down, why he was losing weight and in nearly constant pain. But Chris knew the real reasons; it was a cancer all right, but it was cancer of anger and hatred.

He was most certain the thought had been there since the instant the old man passed out and drove his truck across the double yellow line and murdered Penelope. It had been there long before he learned the driver's name or that Mr. Green would walk because there was no criminal activity committed.

Killing Penelope was not a crime.

Green had "suffered" a heart attack. Chris wondered if the man had really suffered enough.

Chris knew what he would do before this disease that was

killing him struck the death blow.

He would take Mr. Walter Green's life, love, and support. Before he left this world, he would kill Debby Green.

Chris came to, the fog of memory clearing from his head. It was dark. He was still lying on the kitchen floor of the Green's house. In an instant he realized that what had broken through that quiet, black, slumber was the burst of noise. An automobile door had slammed shut.

He rolled over and pain coursed a winding river through him. He was faded and wasted, and there was nothing much left in these muscles at the moment. He pulled himself upright with the help of the kitchen counter. The gun was still in his hand, heavier than ever.

He hoisted himself to his feet, dizzy in the dark and feeling like a blind man. He stumbled to the wall and put his back to it. He felt hot bile rise in his throat.

The front door opened then closed. A light came on in the front of the house. Footsteps clomped over the floors. Heavy steps.

A hand came around the corner in the shadows. The lights came blindingly on and Chris lunged at the figure that stepped into the kitchen. He raised the gun and fired right beside a startled Walter Green's head.

Green fell to the floor, holding his left ear, yelling in pain. Chris fell to his knees beside him, trying to raise the gun again with both hands. He gave it everything he had, but the gun wavered in the air. Chris pulled the trigger a second time, surprising himself that he accomplished the task. The bullet struck the floor far off from the intended target.

Chris coughed up blood then lurched over, landing face down on the floor in a crimson puddle. He labored for breath; he twitched in agony. The gun was lying next to his hand, but his hand wasn't able to obey the command to grab it. He watched his fingers tremble and flex, but that was the extent of their mobility.

"Sweet Jesus," the older man said. The world grew still and silent.

Chris felt hands on him, and then he was being turned over. His eyes fought to focus.

Walter Green wiped blood from Chris's face with his bare hand; he stared from the mess on his shaking hand to Chris lying limp on the floor. "Mr. Linney," Green breathed. "Sweet Jesus, are you okay?"

Chris's arm flopped. He attempted to sit up, to roll over, to do something, but his jelly limbs didn't cooperate and were as coordinated as strings in the wind.

"Penelope," Chris whispered.

Green stood up and disappeared, a blurry vision retreating. Chris turned his head and could make out the gun just inches from him.

Walter Green hurried down the hall to the closet. His ear was still ringing, and he had a hell of a headache. He flung the closet door open and jerked a blanket from the top shelf and a pillow from the bottom corner. He stopped in the bathroom and turned the faucet on full blast. His chest was aching, his heart trying to beat its way out. Walter wet a wash cloth, and then headed back for the kitchen and the intruder on his floor.

He was sure the neighbors heard the gunshots and the police would have been called. *Chris Linney on his kitchen floor.* He was wondering how he was to explain all this when he rounded the corner to the kitchen and stopped. A pillow under his arm, a blanket in one hand, a wet cloth dripping cold water on the floor in the other, and he stood in the kitchen stone cold still.

"Chris...Mr. Linney," Walter said. He felt as if he had eaten a bottle of powder his mouth had become so dry.

Chris had crawled to the door and had made it no further, leaving a trail of smeared blood. He was slumped against the door, gun lying in his limp hand. He had no strength left to even raise his head.

Walter set the pillow and blanket down. "Chris," he knelt, and grimaced as his knees popped. He noticed a quiver run through Chris's body, a trembling in the extremities. Chris's finger itched at the trigger.

Walter wiped blood from the corner of Chris's mouth. His head flopped to the side.

"The police will be coming," Walter said. "Probably an ambulance, Mr. Linney." Walter ran the cool cloth over Chris's lips.

Chris tried to lift the gun. Walter easily took it from Chris's hand, prying it gently away. He stood with a grunt and sat at the table.

Walter looked the gun over and laid it on a homemade placemat. "I thought I knew exactly what I'd say to you if we ever met," he said. "For such a long time I expected you to show up on our doorstep. But there was that part of my mind, too, that was sure you would never show up."

Chris shifted. He was still trembling with pain and weakness, but he managed to raise his head and rest against the door. The room had stopped spinning, now it only swayed like a boat on still waters.

"I'm sorry, Mr. Linney," Walter said. "That's all I know to say. I know it's not enough. I know that. I know that my apologies for what happened, my words, won't bring your wife back."

"Penelope's dead," Chris whispered.

Walter nodded. "She was your world, wasn't she?" The old man's voice broke. He spread his hands over the placemat, tracing the design, the stitches. "My wife made this, made all of them. Little towels, and doilies, and knitted socks for the kids and grandkids. My wife is my world, Chris."

Walter picked the gun up. He studied it intently. "I thought sometimes, if you ever did show up, that you would hit me. You know, punch me on the jaw. I never dreamed you would show up at our house ready to...."

Walter ran his hands over the metal, checked the chamber. "There have been several times in the last few weeks that I've thought of putting a bullet in my brain." He swiveled around in the chair. "If you do it, it would save me the trouble, Mr. Linney."

Chris swallowed down the taste of blood in his mouth. He wanted to talk, but breath was so precious.

"You don't look like you're in any condition to kill somebody," Walter said. "My wife is my world, too. Or she was." He put the gun back on the table. "Or I don't know. Chris, you're the first person I've talked to in the last two weeks that isn't a doctor or a nurse or an insurance rep or...." Walter sighed, deep and long and mournful. "Debby doesn't even know my name anymore." His eyes went beyond the walls for a moment.

Walter tapped his fingers on the gun. "She doesn't even recognize me. My own wife. It's the disease, her mind is gone. Can't dress herself. She can't even remember to eat. My wife is gone, too, see. That's what it feels like. She's in a special home right now, just for people like her. They know how to take care of her. They don't get short with her. I don't mean to, I never have before, but...My Debby is gone, too."

Chris couldn't breathe. His lungs were burning. His stomach twisted, his guts knotted together.

"What do I have left?" Walter asked. "I know how you feel, Mr. Linney. The world is over. Done."

"Yes," Chris coughed.

"I'm truly sorry," Walter said. He held the gun in his hand. "I'm sorry. Killing me won't bring your wife back."

The faint sound of a siren floated through the evening.

"I guess they're coming. Took them long enough," Walter said.

"I miss her so much," Chris said. "So much."

"I know," Walter said. "I do too."

Chris closed his eyes, stray tears seeping free.

"I'm sorry," Walter said. "Nothing can bring them back."

Chris managed to raise his head. "Two…bullets," he said between breaths.

Walter studied the gun. "Yes. Two bullets would be enough," he said as the sirens came closer.

THE END

About the Author: John Robinson is a dad and author living in Middle Tennessee. His work has been published by Crowded Quarantine, Zimbell House, and Jitter. He can be contacted at his Facebook page John Robinson/Literal Remains. (https://www.facebook.com/literal.remains)

Murder of Crows

Thomas Kleaton

The scent of funeral flowers, white lilies and hydrangeas, drifted over to Ernie on the chilling breeze.

Velma's casket lay beneath the sinewy branches of a gigantic live oak tree in the little country cemetery. Together for fifty years, they'd celebrated their anniversary only six months before.

Gold. Ernie twirled the wedding band on his left hand with his right thumb and forefinger. *Fifty years is gold.*

Astro Turf covered the loose dirt of the grave, soil that would be returned after the funeral director's staff lowered Velma away from him forever into the ground. Ernie gave the casket a final cursory glance before shifting his attention to the plot beside it. A small granite cross marked the grave of their only child, Laura, who'd been stillborn in the early years of the marriage. The letters of its single inscription were silted black from the weather:

MY LITTLE ONE SLEEPS

Even now, in his late seventies, Ernie remembered Laura's tiny casket being lowered into the ground beneath the oak tree. A single tear welled up and tracked down his cheek at the thought. Years of weekly visits to sit beside his daughter's gravesite filled his mind. Visits in which he imagined a little girl with birthday cake frosting on her face here, a smiling girl in a Brownie uniform there, a young woman in bridal white, waiting for him to lift her veil and give her a kiss on the cheek as she stood at the end of the aisle with her soon-to-be husband. Visits clouded by grief that had engulfed him for nearly fifty years.

Had Velma known it would be a baby girl?

He shuddered.

Yes. A little bird told me.

The sun was diminishing in the bleak December afternoon, and people were already disbursing, getting into their cars and cranking up the heat. A few more stood around in dark clothing, hugging in groups among the grey headstones. A young girl watched Ernie, curious. He wondered if Laura's ponytails would have been burnt sienna like the ones that fell onto the shoulders of this little girl's frilly black dress, her hands like those clasped together at the girl's waist. He smiled at the girl and then headed over and plopped down in the seat of a dusty Taurus station wagon, their one extravagance, the car Velma would occasionally drive to the town's single Kroger for fresh strawberries and Cool Whip.

Ernie shivered, watching as three crows perched near the top of a scrawny pine tree in the open field opposite him, another group of mourners dressed in black. He wondered if they might be Andrea or Ruby or any of the other women who'd made up that quilting circle Velma always frequented, that circle they called Idle Hands. Ernie gazed at them until they flew off, chattering.

Someone caressed Ernie's shoulder, and he turned. A fiftyish man in black attire stood over him.

"Are you okay, Ernie?" he asked.

No, I'm not okay Mr. Funeral Director. My old girl's gone and there's nothing I can do about it. I do have a mistress, though. Loneliness. She'll be there tonight with the covers turned down; snuggling up to me before I even hit the sheets.

"Don't even want to go home, Vernon," He measured the director with pale-blue eyes. "Takes a while to sink in, I suppose."

"Well, you've got my cell number, if you need someone to talk to." Ernie nodded, solemn, and then drove off down the deserted pavement leading away from the cemetery, the transmission whining as Vernon grew smaller in his rearview mirror.

Ernie paused at the doorway into their bedroom, polishing his eyeglasses with a cotton handkerchief. The house was quiet, the silence interrupted only by the ticking of the clock on the nightstand, the hands resting on eleven p.m. Pecan limbs brushed the house occasionally with gnarled fingers, driven by a wind that was now whipping around the eaves. Their bed was a simple one, constructed of varnished pine. Velma's goldfinch quilt covered it, the one he'd found her dead under two nights ago.

The quilt, sewn especially for her and the baby, had kept Velma warm the night after Laura was stillborn and through the long months of depression after the doctor told her she'd never carry another child to term. It was ragged now, in stark contrast to the opulent quilts with squares of vibrant sapphire and honey that adorned the walls.

Velma had been inconsolable the night Laura died, the night he'd sat at their blue checkered kitchen table and tossed down shot after shot of Wild Turkey, the night he began to suspect there might be a dark side to Velma. Ernie remembered wandering upstairs, Velma sitting there wrapped up in her quilt when he stumbled into the shadowy bedroom, the vanilla scent of her dusting powder intense.

She had been gazing out the window there in the dark, but had turned when she heard him come in, the quilt falling from her shoulders as she got up, screaming at him:

"We just lost a baby and you treat me like this? You no-good drunken bastard! You sot!"

Her eyes had been glowing in the moonlight, just like a deer's eyes caught in the headlights.

115

Just like an owl's.

A vision of a Big Bad Wolf with spiky teeth had come to him then, a wolf dressed in a Blair nightie and hiding behind petite spectacles.

All the better to eat you with, my dear.

Ernie blinked, but it had only been Velma, crying, coming to him with arms outstretched.

He stepped over to Velma's dressing table, his fingers brushing over a photo in a gilded frame. Their wedding picture. Velma's hair was backcombed in the front, cascading into curls at the sides, reminding him of Samantha in *Bewitched*. Another, older picture sat beside it. Ernie's mother. Sarah was young in the photograph, taken the day of his seventh birthday, smiling as she stood beside the chocolate cake she'd made. Sarah, who dropped dead of a brain embolism after lighting his birthday candles.

The faint scent of Velma's Chanel No 5 drifted up to him. He took a deep breath, his chest hitching, remembering:

It was our wedding night and I thought it was the strangest thing... the bluebirds appearing in the cedar trees lining the front yard...the bluebirds that were singing as I carried you across the threshold and into the house...

Ernie turned away as he had on the previous night, knowing he wouldn't be able to sleep here. He might not ever be able to sleep here again. A bloated moon had risen, gleaming through the window across the room.

Good night for a moonlight drive. An idea began to form in Ernie's mind, an old suspicion. *Moonlight drive right out to the cemetery.*

A slight thump rattled the peeling window frame.

Ernie jerked, startled.

A blur of black wings skittered off one of the panes. A crow tottered on the ledge, its vile eyes peeping at him from the dark. Ernie mouthed the words:

Velma...You've come back to me.

It pecked at the window. A slow rapping from the metal

roof above his head completed the discord. Faint at first and then gathering momentum, it echoed through the bedroom like the hollow footfalls of a condemned man shuffling to the gallows. He wondered what would happen if it got in. Ernie gripped his mother's picture, remembering one of her sayings: *"If a bird flies into your house death isn't far behind."*

The ruckus stopped.

Ernie trundled to the bottom of the stairs, favoring his bad leg. He paused to put on his jacket, and then walked out onto the warped boards of the front porch, whistling as frigid air enveloped him. He descended the steps.

And stopped, arrested in his tracks.

He'd left the door of the Taurus ajar when he got home, his thoughts muddled by grief and a lack of sleep. The courtesy light was on and a large crow was perched on the front seat. Ernie waved his arms in a shooing gesture as he jogged to the car and the bird took to the air, something shiny dangling from its beak, one of its wingtips brushing him as it flew past.

There was no key in the ignition.

He went through his pockets, knowing it couldn't be there, knowing he'd left the key in the switch when he got back from the funeral.

He slammed the door and started out across the pasture. A cold orange moon rested on the tops of the Loblolly pine trees behind the barn. Cold air chased the warmth from around his ankles as he hobbled across the pasture, gasping for breath. Sleeping chickens, Leghorns and Rhode Island Reds, scattered before him, indignant.

He heard flapping wings overhead and glanced over his shoulder.

The moon was peeking through purple clouds blown along on the icy wind, clouds hurrying, frantic, with no purpose and nowhere to go. Several crows tottered on that same wind, banking to settle onto the porch, jostling for position on the railings to watch him.

Ernie trudged into the barn and rested on the fender of

his '66 Chevy pickup to catch his breath, the truck he used for occasional trips to the feed store for laying mash and sweet feed. Gertrude, their Jersey milk cow, stared at him indifferently from her wooden stall as Ernie climbed into the cab.

Ernie could hear the birds now, fluttering into the loft, the beating of their wings like a drum inside his head. The crisp scent of hay was everywhere. He snatched the keys from the visor, pumping the gas pedal with his good leg. He turned the key and the red *oil* and *gen* lights came on like the warning signal of a railroad crossing.

The gates are down and the lights are flashing, he thought. *But nothing's coming.*

Only something *was* coming. Ernie could *feel* it.

He twisted the key and the lights went out as the engine sputtered and caught. He pulled out through the weathered barn doors, the headlights cutting a path through the swaying grass leading out to Highway 14. Ernie accelerated, the transmission whining as he shifted from second to third gear and crept up to forty-five. The heater blew warm air over the windshield and across his feet.

Ernie watched the white lines roll past him on his left, thinking about crows and graves, about the time two years before when Bill Pyxell from the Texaco station told him about coming home late one night and passing the same graveyard where Velma now lay, cold and rigid.

"It was the funniest thing, Ernie." He saw Bill's eyes in his mind, magnified behind his thick lenses, the smear of grease above his left eyebrow. *"They'd just buried Andrea Chelsing that afternoon. It was a new moon that night and I came around the curve there just across Prather's Creek and saw a flock of crows clustered over her grave. The sheriff went out there the next morning and found her grave violated. Her marker was toppled and when they dug down to the coffin it was empty. Sheriff blamed it on high school kids."*

Ernie jolted upright when he heard his name, bringing himself out of a daze, but it was only an owl hooting as it swooped down from overhead. Off to his left a clear field sprinkled with cedar trees growing through a barbed wire fence lay bathed in moonlight struggling through the clouds. He turned right onto Anderson Road. He was nearing the cemetery when it began to drizzle, and Ernie turned on the wipers. He was almost to Prather's Creek; he could see the concrete barriers on each side of the bridge, the yellow warning sign posted at the nearer end.

Caution

Bridge Slippery When Wet

He was crossing now, tires clopping over the metal expansion joints of the bridge. A single crow sat on one of the concrete pillars and Ernie's eyes followed it as he passed. He was almost over the bridge when the headlights picked out a flock of vultures huddled together on frosty asphalt where no vultures should've been.

They flew up over his truck as one, and Ernie found himself staring through a windshield blotted out by flapping wings. He slammed on the brake pedal and the old pickup slewed sideways; it righted itself just as the worn Bridgestone tires on the back finished crossing the bridge. The front tire caught the soft shoulder on Ernie's right and he skidded down the incline into the woods. A stream of thoughts ran through his head as he fought for control:

The crow. A crow was on the bridge when the vultures flew up.

The bluebirds flew up out of the cedar trees, singing as I carried you across the threshold.

Velma…You've come back to me.

Ernie covered his face with his hands as the pickup veered into a massive pine tree, nose first. The engine stalled and his seatbelt locked across his lap, throwing him forward. He wondered if maybe they had the ability to call raptors down out of the sky right before his head hit the top of the steering wheel.

Ernie came to half an hour later.

The first thing he became aware of was the cold. He was shivering, his breath puffing out in small clouds. A fine mist coated the windshield. He rubbed his hands together and tried to crank the engine. It spun over a few times but wouldn't catch, the rich scent of gasoline seeping into the cab.

Ernie glanced around, frantic, scanning the side windows and rearview mirror for movement, but there was nothing. He rolled down his window, listening. The woods were silent except for the babble of water churning over the rocks of the creek. He got out and groped around in the truck bed for the battered old Coleman kerosene lantern he kept there, lit it with the Zippo lighter he'd carried since Vietnam, and started walking up the dead grass of the embankment. He turned back almost as an afterthought, heaving aside a bale of hay from the back of the truck to reach what was beneath it.

A shovel.

Ernie ambled over the white line at the edge of the road until he reached the cemetery. He wondered what kind of specter he would resemble should a car suddenly spear him in its high beams.

Her eyes had been glowing in the moonlight. Just like a deer's eyes caught in the headlights.

A minute later he was standing over a cold granite marker, his lantern lighting the words chiseled into it:

Velma Paskell
1940-2016
Dearly Loved Wife of Ernie Paskell

He shone the lantern into the grave. Soil that had been replaced just that afternoon lay scattered in a pile, dislodged as if a large German shepherd had pawed into it, tail wagging, snuffling at the bones that lay beneath. Small tracks covered the loose dirt, and something had tunneled down to the casket. The wooden lid was still intact, but a fissure had been splintered into it, a hole no bigger than a Chihuahua could fit through.

Or a crow.

Ernie leaned over, directing lantern light into the hole. He grimaced and straightened abruptly, his back groaning.

The casket was empty.

He pictured crows cavorting over Velma's grave, saw them clawing at the ground with gritty talons caked with graveyard dirt, their beaks hacking and scratching at the polished elm of her coffin, inviting her to *come out and play with them* under the light of the pagan moon overhead.

Knock, knock, who's there?

Ernie thought about the trinket around Velma's neck, a small pendant hanging from a fine silver chain, tiny, finely-sculpted into the shape of birds' wings, a symbol of a phoenix bird rising from the ashes. The trinket she'd worn their entire marriage, the trinket he'd buried her with.

He thought about how easily the word *circle* would interchange with *coven*. In his mind, the phoenix became a crow wearing a black pointed hat.

He turned to Laura's grave next. He had to know.

He positioned the lantern and then began digging, straining over the shovel. He could feel his pulse thumping in his forehead.

It took him most of an hour to dig down to her coffin. His back flared in protest every time he swung a load of dirt over the edge. The grave smelled of freshly-turned earth, the same robust scent that rolled off his fields when he plowed the dried-out cornstalks under in the fall.

A chill wind sighed through the treetops, rattling the sad remnants of dead leaves in the woods. He'd managed to dig down four feet when the shovel struck wood.

White roots poked from the sides of the grave, capillaries in the black earth. He scraped the loose debris from the lid.

It was undamaged.

Velma and her cronies had hosted a party and his daughter hadn't been invited. Why was she still in her grave?

He pored over the inscription on the marker again.

MY LITTLE ONE SLEEPS.

Hibernating, Ernie thought. *Hibernating like the black bears who've been in their lairs for going on two months now.*

He felt uneasy, as if he were being watched. He could

hear something shuffling around on the dark limbs of the oak tree overhead, stealthy.

Ernie pictured a chrysalis, pale jade or yellow. A new life inside, changing, transforming.

A chrysalis shaped like a coffin.

The voice of Ernie's grandfather spoke up in his mind, advice given during one of their infrequent trips to hunt the White-tailed deer that frolicked over the property.

"Never disturb a hibernating bear, Ernie."

He stared down at Laura's casket, indecisive, and then raised the shovel and smashed the latch.

Wings fluttered overhead when Ernie opened the coffin, like a covey of quail whirring into motion. He caught a glimpse of black shapes above him, theatergoers leaving just before the final act.

Ernie shrank away from the stench that puffed out at him, leaning back on stiff, sore wrists. He reached around and groped for the lantern, swinging its beam into the grave.

A silk embroidered baby dress lay flat in the bottom of the coffin, faded pink.

Ernie leaned over and lifted the hem of the garment, hesitant. It began to move, the upper part of the dress lifting, pivoting at the waist, and Ernie placed his knuckles to his lips. *Butterfly Kisses* began playing in his mind, followed by a cheerful voice echoing over a school loudspeaker:

Okay, folks, time for the daddy-daughter dance!

He swallowed, a scream building in his throat.

The skeleton of a nestling bird peeked at him from the collar, all hollow skull and wing bones.

Ernie shrieked, leaning on his hip and digging his fingers into the loose dirt at the edges of the grave to raise himself up. He turned his face up to white stars, trying to clear his head. He started running in a broken gait, the lantern swinging in a wild arc as he shambled along. His knees collapsed beneath him when he started down toward the truck, and he slid down the embankment, red mud staining his pants. Something screeched overhead and Ernie scrambled towards the door handle. He was still holding onto the lantern when he fell into the seat and jammed the door locks down, his breath burning in his lungs.

He realized then that Velma and the others had just been teenagers or young women curious about the occult, not knowing what kind of forces they were dealing with or what they'd gotten themselves into.

Or maybe they just wanted to be able to fly.

Whatever the women of the quilting circle were, shape shifters or maybe even witches like Samantha in *Bewitched* or the girls in *The Craft*, his daughter was more dangerous.

Far more dangerous.

Another of his mother's sayings popped into his head.

The devil finds work for idle hands.

Velma had kept her secrets from him, but she had loved him. Whatever spark of remembrance Velma held after her transformation had rekindled and they were warning him away from the grave, away from his daughter. Because something had happened to Laura in Velma's womb; something *bad* had gotten into her.

The reason her grave was un-desecrated was simple.

They didn't want to *rouse* her.

Something thumped down on the hood. It was like a flickering shadow in the moonlight, unsteady, and then it assumed a familiar form.

A crow. The thing perched on the hood twisted towards Ernie, and he raised the lantern. It was then he noticed the crook of its vulture-like neck.

Topped by a little girl's head.

Ernie gazed at it, horrified. Strands of black flaxen hair finer than corn silk blew in the wind. The beak, misshapen, gave the ruined head the appearance of a snapping turtle. Eyes that didn't quite line up across its face bored into his with a fierce intensity.

The words the doctor spoke in his ear that cold winter afternoon so long ago came back to him. The words following the news that Velma would never give birth again:

"Maybe it's a good thing she was stillborn, Ernie. She's deformed."

"I love you, Laura." Ernie groped toward it with fingertips that no longer had feeling in them, questioning. The creature hopped forward, eager, and pecked at the windshield. Circles of fractured glass spread like ripples in a pond. He saw no shred of recognition in the thing's eyes, no acknowledgement of the love Ernie had held for it. But he would show her how much he loved her, the only way he knew how.

His little girl had awoken from her nap and she would be hungry.

He reached up and removed an ancient shotgun from the rack in the back window, its barrels sawn off. He thumbed the release lever. Twin brass shot shells gleamed in the light of a white moon. He closed the breech, cocking it.

A smile played across Ernie's lips as he remembered the song his mother would sing as he played with his ABC Blocks, her voice rising into the bright morning sunshine.

"Sing with me." Ernie stared into the thing's black sockets, and began to hum the strains to *I'll Fly Away*.

He placed the barrels beneath the shelf of his chin, could feel them scraping his two-days' growth of whiskers.

Ernie's face took on a faraway look. He could see his mother crumpled on the floor in her pastel print dress, her life snuffed out like the candles lighting his birthday cake. Maybe she would be there, after, her cotton apron still fragrant with Crisco shortening.

Tears welling in his eyes, Ernie placed his finger on both triggers.

And breathed his final wish.

THE END

About the Author: Thomas Kleaton is a freelance horror writer. He has had stories published in The Horror 'Zine, and several anthologies including Cellar Door: Words of Beauty, Tales of Terror; The Horror Zine Magazine Summer 2014;

Spooky Halloween Drabbles 2014 and 2015; and What Has Two Heads, Ten Eyes, and Terrifying Table Manners? He lives in the woods near Auburn University, AL, with his wife, Sheila.

Website: Random Musings http://thomaskleaton.wordpress.com/

Feed My Queen

Joe DiCicco

Jason glanced up at the clock above the bar.

Midnight. On a Tuesday night.

Wednesday morning.

Whatever. It made no difference. What mattered was that it was a weeknight and here he sat at a sleazy little watering hole downtown, drunker than an Irish sailor on shore leave. What was the name of this place anyway? He couldn't recall, nor did he care. He'd never been here before and if someone had told him a week ago he'd so much as step foot in the joint, he would never have believed it.

The barmaid now moseyed back in his direction. She was a pretty thing, couldn't have been much older than twenty-three. Most likely a college girl up in the city, majoring in child psychology or some shit like that. He'd put money down she had a boyfriend keeping the bed warm back home.

"'Nother one?"

Her smile was friendly enough, despite the glassy eyes and dark violet bags hanging just beneath them. He drained the last bit of foam from the longneck before clacking it down on the bar.

Cheap, probably composite.

"Set me up. Another shot, too. Kentucky bourbon." He slid a ten over the sticky bar. "Keep the change."

"Thank you!" It somehow sounded both sincere and pre-recorded.

The burn of bourbon would make him forget. Only for

a moment, but in that moment he would forget he ever knew Maria. That he had ever loved her.

The place was dead, he supposed, even for a Tuesday night.

Wednesday morning.

On the jukebox an old bluesman, Robert Johnson, or maybe Wolfie Terrance, made love to his six strings.

Down the other end of the bar an old drunk sat nursing a pint. He'd been mumbling something to the barmaid every so often, grinning to reveal a nearly-toothless maw. Probably some wet brain on SSD for the past twenty years after hurting his back working construction, or maybe in a drunken motorcycle accident. Probably had a shitty little studio down on Gibbon Street, or more likely at Hanover Homes. Probably spent every night of the week making the rounds, dumping his check on booze and cigarettes, maybe oxys, too. Probably ate cat food so he could save as much as possible for boozing and pill popping. He would stumble out of this dump at closing time and shuffle back to his nasty little pad, which Jason was sure to be full of rats.

You make me sick old man.

On the far end of the room opposite the bar, two men currently shot darts. One looked to be in his mid-twenties perhaps, the other closer to forty. The latter looked like he could be a trucker, though there had been no rig in the parking lot and the two had been here when Jason strolled in around eight. They'd been playing darts all night, screaming murder at the board as if it could hear them. The drunker they got, the louder they got. Probably first-shifters down at PEMTEC.

A couple hours ago a thirty-something yuppie couple had come in, had one round and left.

Couldn't blame them for that.

Jason downed the whiskey, chased it with beer. His chest tightened with the burn, for an all too brief moment before it passed. He would just have to accept it: there was no getting over her.

Four years.

Four years of his life and now it all meant nothing. He had truly, in all honesty, believed she was the one. No one had ever made him feel the way Maria had, and sitting here now in this dive, drowning his woes in the sauce, he understood no one ever would again. He'd once heard how true love comes only once in a lifetime. Maybe not even that often. She was his. His one and only chance at true happiness. All the memories, the songs, the trips up to the city, all the parties, the inside jokes, all the plans they had made for the future; all brought crashing down in one day. How would he be able to go on living in that apartment? How would he be able to come home from work late at night to an empty bed? To see his boots sitting all by their lonesome when for four years they had been accompanied by flip-flops, Converse and heels? All her tapestries, her guitars, all her candles, her clothes...

He felt the tears well up behind his eyes, fought to push them back. He took another swig.

The song on the jukebox ended. It went silent then, but only for a moment. Hearing just the first few notes of what came next, he knew the floodgates were about to open. And no amount of struggling or teeth gritting would hold them closed.

Dog and Butterfly.

This was their song. Just some stupid old song by the band Heart, but Maria had loved it enough to label it their song. She would sometimes sing it to him as they lie in bed, drifting off to dreamland after a long day at work.

Pushing-Forty Possible Trucker rumbled away from the jukebox and Twenty-Something back at the dartboard shouted drunkenly how he loved this song. Jason felt the first tear stream down his cheek. Jumping up, he hurried to the men's room. By the time he got to the grimy sink and looked into the mirror, his face was red and soaked with tears.

Get a grip on yourself dude, you're acting like a pussy! One side of his brain screamed just as the other shrieked back: *It's OK to cry, you know. You love her. You love her more than any woman you've ever loved. More than your own mother even. And you will most likely never see her again. She's probably with him right now, sleeping soundly in his arms...or maybe she woke him with that nibbling on the ear she likes to do...Woke him for a little midnight session...*

Now the tears came streaming, heavier than before. In the mirror he saw his own face twist, distort. He watched his lips pull back, hot breath hissing through gritted teeth. His fists clenched so hard that his nails dug into his palms. He brought them down hard onto the porcelain sink.

Just then the flimsy door of the men's room swung open and Twenty-Something staggered in. For a brief second the two made eye contact. Jason quickly turned, lowering his head.

"Whoa!" Twenty-Something croaked in surprise.

Turning the scummy knob, water hissed from the faucet. Cupping his hands, Jason splashed his face and inspected his eye in the mirror as though he had something in it.

"You alright, bro?" Twenty-Something asked, sounding genuinely concerned.

Jason felt a surge of disgust. *Bro? Do I look like your bro?*

"Yeah, I'm fine, just got some dust in the eye."

After a moment, he turned, keeping his head cocked toward the wall, and shuffled to the exit. Twenty-Something stood there, head wobbling as it turned to follow the stranger.

I bet I'm the most interesting thing he's seen all day, Jason thought. *Hell, maybe even all week.*

Making his way, carefully now, back toward the bar, he noticed someone new had entered the place while he had been on his gentleman's reprieve. Another twenty-something, this one appearing younger than the first. A scrawny bastard, t-shirt and jeans much too baggy for his frame, but he was cocky. That was apparent from the way he took wide steps forward and back while boasting loudly some most likely embellished tale to Aging Trucker.

Jason remembered that arrogance. Wasn't too long ago he carried himself much the same way. Freshly legal, and holy shit did he have something to prove. Probably hadn't even been twenty-one for three months yet. He would get that knocked out of him eventually, hopefully sooner rather than later.

Jason plopped back down onto his stool, hand finding

its way easily back to the bottle. He noticed the codger was missing. For good, judging from the absence of the pint glass on the bar.

Must have stumbled out just as punk-ass stumbled in.

Enjoy your cat food, old man.

The song finally ended. Jason chased it with a nice long swig as if to say Fuck You.

He hadn't suspected a thing. She had said she just wasn't ready. That she was unable to commit the rest of her life to any one person.

Just another lie.

It was all just lies. He had been waiting for her in the parking lot. His best friend since high school. How could he have been so blind? So damned oblivious, not to see this all along? Looking back, the warning signs smacked him in the face; working late, going to be with a friend who was dealing with a particularly nasty breakup. All the classic red flags were there, but damn it all, he had not picked up on one of them. In the end, he had just trusted her too much.

He supposed he would go back to that dark apartment. She would be long gone by now, having taken most of her things. Some of his too, most likely.

Now the twenty-something in the men's room came out. He and Fresh-Baked Twenty-One greeted each other with deafening roars.

Jason craned his neck toward clock: 12:32. He should probably get going.

The three drunk men began a game of darts as Jason ordered one last shot. Why the hell not?

As pretty little college girl (who despite drink after drink, still only reminded him of Maria) poured the whiskey, he clearly heard Mr. I Don't Know What Size Clothes I Wear ask: "Yo, who is that?"

Pushing-Forty Maybe Trucker answered with a "Damned if I know" followed by a belch that had to have come from the very depths of that beer gut. Mr. Men's Room Rendezvous let loose with hysterical laughter as he began to recount how he had walked in on the dude crying like a little bitch in the men's room. At this, all three men broke into thunderous laughter.

Jason ignored this, sliding a five across the bar. It was time to take his leave. The men watched with apparent interest as he drained the shot, set it down hard onto the bar.

"Thank you!" Miss Barmaid had an ear-to-ear smile that seemed genuine enough. He stood, swiveled away from the bar, offered a sorry attempt at a return smile. He could feel the men's eyes staring him down; cold, glassy.

Outside, the air was warm and still, smelling faintly of stale cigarette smoke. He stopped halfway down the steps to light a cigarette beneath the glow of a neon red and blue Open sign. Once lit, he took a deep drag, making his way down the remainder of the steps, hand on the rail for good measure. In the back of his mind he knew what he was about to do was pure stupidity. But that part of his brain that handled better judgment was drowned in a soupy mixture of booze, heartache and a deep gut feeling that things could not get any worse. In the split second between the screen door kicking open behind and hearing the hostility in that voice, he realized they were about to.

"Yo, bro! What's wrong, you don't like it here?"

Jason turned. Sure enough, there stood Fresh Out The Oven Twenty-One, brow turned down angrily, eyes glazed. Behind him stood the fat trucker, shoulders arched, face scowling under woodland-camo baseball cap. Just a week prior, Jason may have taken the bait, but tonight he was too drunk and too depressed. He simply turned back around, continued to his car.

A deeper voice now, older, huskier: the trucker. "Hey, faggot! We're talking to you!"

He continued walking.

"Yeah, you better keep on walking, bitch!" Freshly Twenty-One again. "I better not catch you hitting on my girl again! If I see your bitch-ass here again, I'm 'gonna kick it in!'"

Jason stopped not three feet from his Chevy. He stared for a moment at the moths fluttering in the hazy yellow light of the streetlamp overhead.

Why not? What did he have to lose?

He turned back to face the bar entrance. "She your girl?"

"Yeah she is, so just back your gay ass up."

"Good for you. Just treat her right. You never know when it could end. One day she just might take off with your best friend." He turned back to the car, reaching into his pocket for his keys.

From the top of the steps behind: "What?! What the fuck did you just say?"

He had gotten the door open, was about to sit down when he felt the dull pain to the back of his head. Falling forward against the roof of the car, more blows followed, one after another.

"Yeah, what now, punk-ass bitch?!"

Jason slid down onto the hood, rolling over as he did. Twenty-One began to swim wildly, landing a poorly placed punch onto the windshield. With the kid shrieking in pain, or maybe anger, Jason saw his opportunity. Darting to the right, he attempted to steady himself, his vision swimming in thick liquid. The punk was holding his fist, spouting curses. Jason lunged forward, fists carrying all his weight behind them. One placed on the left side of the punk, knuckles digging upward into the ribs. Twenty-One let go a raspy Ahhht! before Jason silenced it with a hook to the jaw. The kid went down hard on his ass and stayed there.

In this moment, Jason realized he needed to be far from here. The shouting would have woken someone in the apartment complex across the street, and it would be a matter of minutes, possibly even seconds, before the cops rolled up. The suddenly not-so-tough-guy lay dazed on the pavement, blood trickling from his lip. He had become stone silent.

Whatever, that was just fine. Jason wanted nothing more to do with this scene. He staggered the few feet to the car and was about to slip into the driver's seat when he heard the huffing of a large man just to his left. This was followed by the scraping of engineer's boots on the pavement.

Then, the deeply venomous: "Faggot motherfucker!"

He felt yet more blows to the back of the head, these heavier than the first. The ripe stench of BO filled his nostrils. He felt meaty arms attempting to bar his own in a full nelson. He knew dully, throbbingly, that if this fat-fuck was to get hold of him, he'd be ten miles up shit creek, not a paddle in sight.

Mustering a burst of booze-strength, he yanked his arms forward. He jerked around as he did this, leaned back against the hood. Growling through gritted teeth, he brought up his boot, launched it squarely into fatty's substantial beer gut. Mr. Trucker or Maybe Factory Laborer fell to his knees, releasing a cascade of light beer, fries and corndogs. Jason used this moment to catch his breath. Just as he was lifting himself off the now nicely-dented hood of his Chevy, a booze-saturated war cry bellowed from atop the bar's front steps.

"Motherfucker! I'll kill you!"

He had just enough time to think *Oh, come on!* before Mr. Gentleman's Room Rendezvous came charging, fists flailing madly. Jason saw all of this in a drunken blur, saw the colors flashing before his eyes, red and yellow, blue and orange. Next thing he knew, he was the one on the pavement, sneaker-clad foot battering relentlessly at his chest. He did not feel the pain. If he was lucky he would feel it tomorrow.

He knew however, that he had to get to his feet. Had to get to his car and get out of Dodge. The barrage of kicks kept coming. If he didn't pick his ass up off the concrete, he might very well die here tonight.

Fat Mr. Trucker was dry heaving now, beginning to bring himself to one knee. If that big bastard got to his feet it would be game over.

Despite the sneaker still jabbing into his ribs, he found one last bit of strength. Rolling to his right, he hopped to his feet, nearly losing his balance in the process. Gentleman's Room Rendezvous was still swinging, but in his own inebriated state, misjudged his distance and as he failed to connect a wild swing, he went down hard onto one knee. Realizing what Jason meant to do, Gentleman's Room Rendezvous bellowed, "Grab him! Grab his ass!" Mr. Trucker was beginning to stand now, breathing heavily, shirt stained with vomit.

Jason made a mad dash the few feet to the car and jumped in. Slamming the door shut, he flicked the lock just as the fat man grabbed the handle.

"Open up! Open this door NOW! I'll kill you, faggot!" He was slamming his massive fist into the window so hard that blood from his cracked knuckles now smeared across it, clouding its view. Through the windshield, Jason saw Gentleman's Room Rendezvous dart around the front, hell bent for the passenger door. In an instant he leaned across and clicked the lock. A split second later Gentleman's Room Rendezvous was frantically trying the handle, throwing fists into the window much the same way as his buddy on the driver's side.

Fishing his keychain from his pocket, Jason kicked the engine to life, simultaneously throwing the stick into reverse. Fatty and Gentleman's Room Rendezvous came barreling after, roaring like berserkers charging a battlefield long ago, their fists slamming onto the now substantially damaged hood.

Once in the street, Jason looked over to see the barmaid kneeling over young Mr. Not So Tough Guy, who still sat on the pavement, dabbing blood from his lip and studying it. It looked like he was asking what the hell just happened.

Popping the stick into first gear, Jason tore down Billings Street, meaning to get as far away from that dive and those drunken bastards as possible. One last glance in the rearview revealed Fat Man had given up, but Gentleman's Room Rendezvous had chased the car about two hundred feet. He had finally given up, both hands raised in one-finger farewell gestures for good measure.

Head pulsating, he turned onto Chestnut, meaning to get out of town and take the back roads home. If someone had called the cops, they would be on their way. Though much quicker, Main Street was far too risky.

From Chestnut he hung a right onto Anderson, followed by another right onto Swisher, eyes darting from the road to the rearview, anticipating those red and blue bubble gums. About three miles down Swisher, he took a left onto County Road Seventeen. He would travel about twenty miles on 17, then hang back around into town via DeWolf, careful to stay at the speed limit the entire time. From DeWolf it would only be about a half mile to Countryman where his apartment complex was.

Seventeen was certainly backroad. Mostly wilderness on both sides, the few houses out this way were miles apart. Not another vehicle in sight. That was good.

A couple miles down, he began to catch his breath. Reaching up, he touched the back of his head, gently. Feeling the sharp pain burst to life, he yanked it back. That pain rolled out in a tidal wave, shot from the top of his head down his neck, where it blossomed across his shoulders in hot tendrils. He would be feeling this in the morning. The nape of his neck was sticky with drying blood, which he could feel staining the backside of his shirt. Drunken bastards. How could he have been so stupid to play right into their little game? This day could not get any worse, of that Jason was now certain.

Rolling down the blood-smeared window, he cocked his head out into the warm night air. No sirens, at least none that he could hear. That was also good. He could feel himself sobering up a bit now.

He thought of an old Doors song then. Was it L.A. Woman? Or maybe Roadhouse Blues? *"Keep your eyes on the road, your hands upon the wheel."* Will do Jim, will do.

He had caught his breath now. All he needed to do was get home, drop into bed, and crash. The doozy on the back of his head would need to be cleaned and disinfected, the blood would need to be scrubbed off the car...and how the hell was he going to get those dents...

Holy shit!

The windshield spider-webbed as something
some animal oh god please some animal
rolled off it, tumbling over the roof.

He slammed on the break, driving his chin hard into the

wheel. The tires screamed across the blacktop. He was able to cut the wheel just sharp enough to stop not six inches shy of the ditch.

"Son of a cocksucker!" Fresh blood rushed from his chin down the front of his shirt. He gritted his teeth against the white-hot pain that now seared down his neck. "What in the ever-loving shit was that?"

Please be an animal oh Christ PLEASE

Finding himself once again chasing his breath, hands glued to the wheel, he almost thought it had looked like...

Nope not possible not even when drunk

A giant bat.

Craning his neck with considerable effort, he looked out the back window. Something dark and

Oh god

human sized sprawled motionless on the highway, illuminated in the red glow of the brake lights.

Dead sober now, he pushed open the door, standing carefully. Slowly, cautiously, he stepped closer. Coming within ten feet of the dark slump, his heart free-fell into an abyss that surely had no bottom. Feeling a wave of cold terror wash over him, he turned, just as every ounce of liquid he had consumed that evening came rushing forth in a tidal wave. Here on the center line of Country Road 17 lay a young woman.

A young woman who was most certainly dead. And naked. For whatever reason, this woman lying here in the center of the road was bare naked, her skin so fair it nearly reflected the headlights.

Tears stinging his eyes, blood and vomit staining his shirt, his mind raced on what to do next. He had to be sure...

Kneeling over the body out here in the dark, he checked for a pulse.

Her skin is ice cold! His brain screamed. No pulse. He placed his hand on her chest. She was not breathing.

Oh god oh god oh god

He was well over the limit. Vehicular manslaughter. They would nail him to the wall.

Oh fuck oh fuck oh fuck

He had to get out of here.

No!

He couldn't leave her out here. Not like this. He had to get her to a hospital.

But she's already dead!

His stomach locked up. He turned just as another wave purged forth.

What the hell was she doing out here in the middle of nowhere? Christ I didn't even see her!

When the heaving had finally stopped, he knew he must be empty. Getting to his feet, he stumbled over to the car, propped himself against the hood. He closed his eyes.

Just go! Get the hell out of here!

No!

Then turn yourself in. You know they will find you eventually. Forensics and all that. DNA. You touched her. They can match the damage on your car to the damage on her body. Can even tell the angle you hit her at and how fast you were going. Might as well turn yourself in and try for fifteen years instead of twenty-five.

Oh shit oh shit oh shit

I'll drive her to the hospital and tell them I found her like this.

Hah! Are you drunk or just stupid? Go on ahead, go in there covered in blood and reeking of liquor and tell them you just happened upon her by the roadside. I'm sure they will believe you. Might as well tell them Bigfoot and the Loch Ness Monster came out of a flying saucer and killed her with laser beams from their assholes.

OK. I'll drive her to the hospital, dump her in front of the ER and tear ass out of there before anyone sees me...

Cameras my friend, cameras. They will get the plate number, make and model, maybe even a nice view of your dopey face. Sun won't even be up yet and you'll get that knock on your door...

He had to do something. Whatever that may be, he knew he could not stand here in the middle of the highway, thumbs all a' twiddlin'.

Taking a deep breath, he bent down, lifting her into his arms. She was surprisingly light for dead weight. He carried her to the car, set her down carefully across the backseat. Illuminated by the ceiling light, he finally got a good look at her. His breath nearly stopped.

She was the most beautiful woman he had ever laid eyes on.

She appeared to be in her early-twenties, no older than twenty-five, max. And she didn't even have any wounds! No horrible gashes or gnarled limbs, not even a drop of blood. And her face! No expression of fear or shock to betray her final moments. She actually looked peaceful, almost as if she wasn't dead at all, just...

Sleeping

Her hair fell down around her breasts, shined a bright crimson silk. Her skin was flawless, not so much as a scratch on that peaceful face. He could not get over how white that skin was. It reminded him of virgin snow in the cold blue light of a January morning.

Stepping back, he shut the door. This just didn't make any sense. He was going fifty-five when he hit her.

Or did she hit me?

She should look like she'd been put through a meat grinder. Instead she looked...Perfect.

He felt a sliver of hope just then. She showed no signs of trauma. No one would ever suspect she had been hit by a car...

Maybe she was already dead when I hit her? How is that possible?

He did not have a clue. But he had to be gone from here.

Plopping down into the driver's seat, he turned the key, praying the engine would start. It did. Thank God for small favors. Slapping the stick in reverse, he straightened the car out, gunned it down seventeen. Putting miles behind him, his eyes darted from the road, to the beautiful young woman lying dead in the backseat.

No, I need to bring her to the hospital. I'll tell them I found her like this, on the side of Seventeen. Maybe she OD'd. Who the hell knows?

Up ahead, the lights from town shown beyond the trees. Only a few miles left to go. He began to relax, ever slightly.

That's when he felt the blade press into the soft flesh

below his chin.

Eyes darting to the rearview, his first thought was that he must have died when he hit the girl.

What he was seeing now could not be real.

Eyes, piercing and green.

Cat's eyes.

They appeared to be glowing faintly in the darkness. Illuminated by the moonlight through the windows was the pale, strikingly beautiful face of the young woman, mere inches from his own. And this was no knife held against his throat, but a

Nope I'm dreaming wake up wake up wake up

hook, claw...Shiny and black...Attached to a blood-red wing. Leathery. A bat's wing.

Oh god wake up please please PLEASE

"Slow down and I'll slit your flesh."

That voice...Soft, like a child's. But those eyes! Captivating, yet somehow...

Predatory

He was at a loss for words. Finally he did manage to speak, his voice dry, quivering. "I...How did you...I thought you were dead!"

That face, like cemetery marble. Those eyes, like embers in a witch's hearth. "I am."

He was at a complete loss now. He tried to turn his head, the knife

Hook claw

pressed harder, forcing him to turn back to the road.

He swallowed hard. "Are you...Are you hurt?"

No reply.

"Damn. What the hell were you doing out there? I didn't even see you, you know. Are you sure you're not hurt?"

"Why didn't you leave me for dead?"

"What? I couldn't do that. Look, I'll take you to the hospital downtown. It's not far, a couple more miles and we'll be in town."

He felt the blade press harder yet against his throat. A

139

warm trickle ran down his neck.

"How about I just tear out your throat and leave you for dead?"

He pressed down harder on the gas pedal. "Look, ma'am, I'm sorry. I swear I didn't even see you.

It's dark out tonight and—"

The young woman scoffed. "Where were you taking me? To dump me in the forest like so much garbage?"

"No! No, I swear! I was taking you to the hospital."

"Lies!"

He felt unbelievable strength behind that arm.

Wing

It was hard to believe that strength belonged to this young woman. He believed she really could do these things if she saw fit.

She inched her face closer, sniffing. "You reek of liquor. Do you always operate this machine in drunken haste?"

"No! No never, this is the first time, honest."

Her lip curled up in a cruel smile. "Inebriate fool."

He felt tears welling up in his eyes. "...Are you the devil?"

The young woman appeared confused. "I suppose I can be."

Jason thought he knew what was happening. He supposed it was time for a confession.

"Truth is, I hardly ever drink...I sure as shit would not have been out drinking tonight if I hadn't found out this afternoon that...that my girlfriend was fucking my best friend. Well, ex-best friend." He let go a hack. There was nothing but contempt in it. "I had just gotten the ring. Took me six months to save up for that damned thing. I'd had it all planned out, too. I was going to propose on—"

He felt the pain only for second, like a razor held over a fire. Then blood was spurting in all directions. On the dash, on the windshield, in his eyes. He felt the flesh tear away, catching a brief glimpse in his rearview of the demon-woman, eyes now black as coals, face splattered with his blood. He saw her teeth; A row of long incisors ripping into his flesh, chewing it, savoring it. His hands fell away from the wheel, causing the car to veer right. It slammed hard into the ditch before coming to rest on a lonely stretch of seventeen, less than a mile from the Pine Lake village limit.

Sprawled across the passenger seat, blood still spurting from the gaping wound in his neck, Jason heard the door open behind him. As his vision began to darken, he felt himself being pulled out, lifted into slim yet incredibly strong arms. In those last few seconds before the darkness took him, he felt a sensation of rising, of leaving ground. He watched with fading consciousness as the trees grew smaller far below. The streets and buildings of town became like a photograph, a miniature, illuminated in the yellow glow of the streetlamps. High he rose into that dark sky, then...

Nothing.

Where am I? What...What is this?

He attempted to sit up, but the pounding in his head put him back down flat. He touched his neck. A raw, sticky mess. Dried blood, black in the pale moonlight seeping in from above, it stained his hands and clothing. Then he remembered...

Not possible. Must have been a dream. But where the hell am I? It smells like a crypt...

"Ah, about time you awoke. I fancy my meat warm."

Her.

There she stood, but a few feet away, body perfect and full, skin a perfect alabaster. She seemed to glide rather than walk toward him. He could only watch her approach, knowing full well what she meant to do, yet being utterly powerless to stop it. He heard a growl, like a lion, deep within her chest. He watched in stupid amazement as her mouth opened, widened beyond what seemed physically possible. Countless rows of jagged little teeth were revealed then in that cold moonlight. She moved with speed that was beautiful, blinding. This time there was no pain at all, only a deep warmth that ran down his neck, into his chest.

A few feet away, across this damp, ancient tomb lay the festering remains of what looked like a girl, maybe a teenager. The skin was a sickening grey, pulled tight across the bones, mouth forever open in a dying scream. Next to her, propped against the stone wall, was an even older corpse, this one not much more than a skeleton. Its bones were heavy with crypt-dust.

He felt the last life draining out of him. His eyes turned up to the dust-covered window, high up near the ceiling. The sky was beginning to lighten now, cold, uncaring. In this final moment, he was vaguely surprised at what he felt. Not anger, not despair, but gratitude. Gratitude and a warm comfort. He began to slip back into the abyss, this time for good. With his last ounce of strength, he reached up and ran his blood-stained fingers through her silken hair.

Feed, my queen. Feed.

THE END

About the Author: Joe DiCicco is a 31 year old author from New York, who writes horror, thriller, and dark fantasy and sci-fi. He has a degree in environmental conservation and is an avid nature and animal lover. When not writing he enjoys music, cooking, astronomy, and spending time outdoors. His story, *Feed My Queen*, was previously published in 2013 by Vamptasy Publishing. He also has a fantasy short, *The Last Druid*, published in the *Mystical Bites* anthology by Crushing Hearts and Black Butterfly Publishing, as well as a horror short *Her Nook*, published at innersins.com. He has another horror short, *Amped*, that will be published in Death Wound Zine in April of 2016.

ART IMITATES DEATH

SEAN TAYLOR

"LOVE, any devil else but you
Would for a given soul give something too."
—John Donne, "Love's Exchange"

"No Really, I'm Fine," Mark said, putting the cell phone in the empty passenger seat. "You don't have to come up. I'll be perfectly fine."

"I worry about you." Melinda's warmth was evident even over the lousy connection. "You're all alone up there. It was one thing to be on the mountain when you and my sister…" Her voice fell away, then grew warm and strong again. "Well, when there were two of you… But now that you're all by yourself, it's got to be a little creepy."

The road twisted ahead of him with only the lights from his BMW to help him follow the serpentine mess of roughly paved gravel paths. Like something from his past, growing up in southern Georgia, only with gravel instead of red clay. Drive for miles and see nothing but woods and fields, and then— boom—suddenly a bed and breakfast or a fishing lodge jumps out at you from around the next tight curve. Any minute now, his home away from home, his two-story art studio would do the same, where she would be waiting for him.

"I'm a sculptor, Melinda." He grinned at the phone even though he knew she couldn't see it. "I'm supposed to like solitude. Remember? Besides, I've got a new project to keep me occupied for several weeks."

There was a long silence.

"Okay, but you call me at least once a week, and if you get lonely, just know that I can be up there in about an hour and a half. We could grab some dinner at that mom and pop seafood buffet."

"Bill and Vera's Seafood Shack."

"That's the one."

"Yeah. That was one of your sister's favorites."

Melinda coughed and cleared her throat. "Well, we don't have to eat there."

"No," he said, picking up the phone from the seat. "It's fine, really. But not for a few weeks. I really want to finish this new project and then I'll call you up for a weekend and show her off to you. I think you're going to love it. It's my most personal work so far. I'm really putting a lot of love into it."

"Okay, if you're sure."

"I'm sure. Don't worry about me."

A deer ran in front of him and he hit the brakes, dropping the phone and sending it careening into the floor. "Hold on," he shouted.

Melinda's voice suddenly sounded like a fairy stuffed under a pillow. The phone had probably been jostled under the seat. He could hear her but couldn't make sense of the muffled squeals and squawks.

"Just a minute!" he yelled, and spun the car to a stop.

He leaned over and dug under the seat until he found the phone and held it up to his ear. "Got it. Sorry about that."

"What happened?"

"A deer."

"You okay?"

He laughed. "After what we've been through the past year, you're worried about a deer crossing in front of my car? Talk about a loss of perspective."

He heard his sister-in-law laugh too. "But you are okay, right?"

"Yeah. Wasn't even close."

Something rustled loudly in the bushes a few feet away,

and Mark jerked his head sideways to get a look. But it was too dark and the headlights were facing the wrong direction. "Damn," he said and leaned over to open the dashboard pocket. Groping blindly, his fingers searched for the flashlight he kept there. When they didn't find it, he remembered leaving it in the trunk after using it down at the cemetery when he had visited the gravesite a few days earlier.

"Mark?"

"Hang on. There's something in the bushes."

"One of *them*?"

"Probably not. But after everything, it's just got me jumpy, that's all."

"Then get the hell out of there and come home."

He shook his head. "No. Until I get my head around all this and finish my new project, this is home."

Melinda's silence told him how frustrated she was at him. But she wouldn't understand.

"Really, I'll be fine. I'm sure it's just rabbits or something."

He listened for the rustling again, but there was no sound at all. Just eerie silence.

"See, it's gone already."

She still said nothing, only heaved heavy, angry breaths into the phone.

"I've got a shovel, and I know where my towel is," he said with a smirk.

"You big geek," she said with a giggle. "We never could change your mind when you had it made up."

"What can I say? I'm stubborn."

"Listen, Mom and Dad would like to see you too. They wanted me to tell you that you're still family regardless."

"They're sweet. Tell them I love them too."

"You tell them."

He sighed. "I will. But I've got so much to do first."

"Mark?"

"Yeah?"

"I wasn't kidding about dinner. I'd really like for you to take me out when you're ready." She took a long breath he could hear over the phone. "I know it's forward and after, well, after my sister's illness, most people would think I'm some kind of whore to even bring it up."

"Not now, Melinda."

"When, then?"

"Please."

"Okay. I'll give you more time, but if you don't invite me up within the next month, I'm coming anyway, whether your project is finished or not." She laughed, and he thought it sounded forced. She was so much like her twin sister, and he had certainly been able to read the truth behind her laughs too. "Deal?"

"Deal. Let me let you go. I want to focus on these nightmare curves up here, so I don't end up in a ditch."

"Be careful. I'm serious."

"I'm hanging up now."

"'K. Bye."

"You're nuts."

"Runs in the family. Be careful."

"Will do. Bye."

He pressed the red button and tossed the phone in the passenger seat again. Melinda had been good to him after the funeral, but even as comforting as she had been and would like to be, he couldn't be distracted.

The woman he loved waited for him in his studio. And he had already been waiting months to see her again.

The stitches were barely visible. Melanie's legs were gone, that was true enough, but the skin had still been intact enough to make the cuts almost seamless. Only a faint red line covered by the criss-crossed black thread gave any indication she hadn't been born without them. And body paint and makeup would cover even those marks. She would be perfect again soon.

Mark traced his fingers along the stitches like he had once traced them along Melanie's lips when they were making love—as though time were limitless and to rush the act of skin touching skin would taint the act and reduce it to mere sex.

"Mmmm."

Melanie was stirring from sleep. She'd probably wake up cranky again as well. He wasn't sure if her increased irritability were an effect of losing the limbs or from the degeneration of tissue, but it didn't matter. She was his wife, and no matter what she had gone through, whatever nightmare has sought to claim her, he would steal her from anything that dared to take her—even death.

"Mark."

Even as soft as it was said it wasn't a question.

There were still traces of the voice he remembered. Something in the timbre if not the texture or the octave. That and the quick way she ended the 'k' at the end of his name when she was angry.

"Right here, honey."

"I can't feel my legs. I can't feel my fucking legs."

He stroked the side of her face, ignoring the roughness caused by the dehydration of her skin. "We talked about this, remember?" he said, pulling his hand away as she angled her head toward it and sniffed to get his scent.

"What the hell did you do to me? Where are my damn legs?"

He continued stroking her, his fingers working into the matted mess that was left of her hair. "I cut them off. They were no good anyway, all rotten and malignant from the sickness. We talked about this before at least a hundred times. It was the only way to save the rest of you."

"You cut off my legs?" Melanie sounded as if she were about to cry. Even with her mangled voice he could still tell. She was his wife, the other half of his soul as they had promised in their vows, and if anyone could tell she was going to cry, he could tell. She was still his goddamn wife.

"I had to, sweetheart."

"All of them?"

He smiled at her. "Yeah, honey. All of them. All the way up to the joint." And he had done a damn fine job he thought to himself, a damn fine job indeed.

"Did you, did you have to —" He could hear the anger in her voice starting to subside, fading into a sad sort of curiosity.

He lifted her head to face him, eye to eye, but by the temples, not by the jaw—not yet. She wasn't ready. "We talked about it, all of it, but I'll tell you again, sweetheart, a hundred more times if I have to. The disease ate away your legs so bad that they were dead. There was no saving them. I would have if I could. You know that."

She shook her head and opened her eyes wide. "I know that?" Then she nodded. "Yes. I know that. I'm sorry. I know that." She blinked once, twice, then shook her head again and smiled at him, a lopsided motion that revealed the torn muscles of her jaw line that showed through her shredded lower lip. "I just have so much trouble remembering things lately."

Mark leaned in and kissed her forehead, her perfect and soft forehead, the first of the skin he had managed to rehydrate and return to life. "It's okay, baby. We've got all the time in the world."

"Mark?"

"Yeah, sweetie?"

"I'm really cold."

"I know."

"Aren't you?"

He grinned. "Not really. I've got the heat up and the fire going in the living room. I'm actually sweating a little bit." He pulled up his shirt to show her the wet stains soaking his chest.

"Oh."

"Yeah."

"I'm so cold though." She coughed, and a bit of dried blood dropped onto the oak floor.

"It's okay. You'll probably feel like that a while." He stepped toward the door separating his studio from the living room. "Want me to add another log on the fire?"

"Please," she said, then added weakly after another cough. "I'm so tired."

"Take a nap then, sweetie. I've got some work I need to

finish anyway."

"When can I see it?" Melanie lifted her head and looked up at the ceiling. "Something's different."

Mark leaned against the door frame. "When I'm done. You know the drill. Nobody sees any new project until I'm happy with it. Artist's prerogative. We're all pretentious bastards that way."

She didn't respond, only kept staring up at the ceiling, an angled frame of pine posts that gave the studio the look and feel of a wilderness cabin retreat to set it off from the rest of the house. "Something's different."

"I took out the skylight and roofed over it." He tapped on the door frame. It gave a dull wooden thunk for each tap. "Didn't feel safe after all the bad weather lately. Thought we needed something more solid."

"Oh." She didn't look down.

"Besides," he said as he felt along the wall for the light switch. "We get plenty of light from the windows."

She craned her neck to see outside but found the curtains drawn, covering the windows and cutting her off from the world outside the house. "I can't see the trees."

"It's dark, silly," he said and flipped off the light. "There's nothing to see out there anyway, and keeping the shades closed keeps out the cold."

"Mark?"

He touched his finger to his lips. "Sleep for now, honey. I'll check on you in a little bit."

He turned and pulled the door closed behind him, heard it click and slumped back against it and let himself fall to the floor in a heap. He stared ahead at the fireplace. Nothing burned in spite of what he'd told her.

Her chills were something he could never repair. Not even if he burned the whole damn house to the ground around them. And no matter how beautiful she might eventually become again.

His heart pounded in his ears, no longer confined to his chest. He hated lying to her, but she'd never understand that it was all necessary. If he hadn't had the courage to… *alter* her then they'd have never been able to be together again like they had promised. Without his work to perfect her, she'd have been corralled into a facility like the others. No. It was the only way. And after he was done, no one could ever tell that she had been something foul and unclean and murderous.

He was an artist, and she would be not only his bride again, but his greatest work.

The morning coffee had sat too long while he showered and it had grown cold, but he drank the oversized ceramic mug of it in a few long draws anyway then set the mug down again on the breakfast table. It sat beside the five-piece set of pottery chickens—one hen, a rooster, and three chicks—that occupied the center of the table, a gift from Melanie's parents during a surprise visit. The mug itself was a gift from Melanie, an oversized one with a Frankenstein monster on the side. The creature's arms joined together at the hands to make a handle that even Mark's thick fingers could fit through comfortably.

"Shit," he said and pushed the mug away. "What are you doing, Mark? You're crazy to think this will work, you know that?" He tapped his forehead three times and pressed against it hard enough to feel the pressure against his skull. Then he grinned before answering himself. "But what choice do we have? Really, what other chance in hell do we have?"

He grabbed the mug again and filled it up with cold coffee.

"Shit. I suppose I could move on and make a new life, but a promise is a promise, right?"

He lifted the coffee to his lips took a long swallow. No cream. No sugar. No anything. Just cold black ooze hitting the back of his throat and draining down thick and slow.

He downed two more mugs of the murky stuff before working up the courage to enter the studio.

Melanie was awake and waiting for him. She smiled instead of asking about her legs. That, at least, was a good sign. Perhaps they'd have a good day today. No slip ups. No reversions. No descents into what the sickness had done to her before he cut away the infected parts.

"Good morning, sunshine," he said, making his way to the curtains to open them. As he did the sunlight spilled in, bathing Melanie's form in a glow not unlike that of a Renaissance Madonna. Her torso hung suspended on the rack he had made for her weeks ago. Limbless, her body resembled a dressmaker's dummy more than a human being.

The thick cotton gown he had draped over her only made the resemblance more complete. There was no sense in freaking her out if she saw all the changes to her body. Soon though, soon she wouldn't need the gown to hide her.

"You look happy," Melanie said, craning her neck to follow him around the perimeter of the studio.

"I am." Mark stopped and took a deep breath. "Being around you always makes me happy."

"Guess what?" she said.

He opened the last of the curtains with a wide flourish that almost slipped into a flirty bow. "What's that?"

"I remembered this time."

"Remembered what?"

"About my legs. Not at first, but after a minute or two. I didn't get mad though. I made myself remember so I wouldn't be mad at you this time."

He touched the side of her face, and she didn't twist to sniff him. "That's my good girl," he said. He let his fingers linger longer than usual. "I don't like it when we fight."

"You know what though?"

"What's that, honey?"

She turned toward his hand and he jerked it away.

"Don't want a kiss this morning?"

"Oh."

He slowly put his hand close to her face again. She kissed it, and he pulled it away again.

"That's nice," he said.

"Glad you like it. It feels nice to me too. What little I can feel, I mean. It's like my arms and face are numb."

He grinned. "Like that Cosby skit about the dentist. *Fiber* in my *mouboth*. You remember that one, right?"

She scrunched up her face. He let her think. The last time they'd watched the comedy special had been at least a year before the sickness got her, and a memory that old might be hard to track down quickly. Might be impossible for all he knew. It depended on what the damn sickness had done to her brain. After nearly a minute though, he interrupted her attempt.

"It's all ri—"

"Four years old," She interrupted and coughed, but he thought it sounded like she was trying to laugh. He let himself believe that anyway. "That's the one with the kid who was four years old."

He grinned this time, a full-on, warm up the heart grin that he hadn't let himself feel in weeks. "That's it."

He walked up to her and threw his arms around her chest and squeezed. Only the cracking of a rib beneath him made him remember to relax his grip. She leaned into him and when her face touched his shoulder, he let go and stepped back.

"That was nice," she said.

"Yeah, but I have to be careful." He wiped some of her dead skin from his chin. "I might hurt you still if I'm not careful."

"Oh," she said and her eyes drooped in disappointment. "Anyway, what I wanted to tell you was that I think I'm getting better. At least my appetite is coming back. I'm starving."

"That's good," he said. "I only fixed some oatmeal and coffee this morning, but I could make some for you, if you want."

"Got any bacon instead? Or maybe some of the deer sausage we had ground?"

"Think so, but don't you want to take it easy on your stomach before hitting a big breakfast whole hog like that?"

"Not the big breakfast, just the meat. I'm really in the mood for meat for some reason. Must need protein after resting so much."

He nodded and stroked her face again. "Sure, but let me

check you out first."

"Whatever you say, honey."

Her eyes followed his fingers as best she could while he inspected her face and chest. No more degeneration of tissue, but no real growth either. And the grafted skin was dying too. If re-growing her original skin or grafting new skin wasn't the answer, he would have to look into other options, even those from his art kit rather than the little surgical remedies he could glean from the Internet.

He lifted the gown and checked the new stitches along the joints of her shoulders. The arms had come off easily enough during the night as she slept, but she hadn't noticed yet—thank God for that—and she must still be feeling phantom sensations as if the limbs were still there. Thank God for that too. Let her believe they were there until he had to tell her the full and horrible truth.

If he had thought the new Melanie had favored a dressmaker's dummy before, then now, with her arms removed to go along with her missing legs, he was more convinced than ever. He even corrected his previous comparison.

Before, he realized, she had been a Roman goddess, a Venus whose legs had been ravaged by time. Only now she was a dressmaker's dummy. Or perhaps she had become a bust. He laughed and she looked at him, her eyes wide and the skin where her eyebrows had been lifted high and arched.

"What's so funny, honey?" she said.

He shook his head. "Just an old art joke from college."

"So tell me."

"It's about busts."

"Like boobs?"

"Well, not the original use of the word, but the boob connection is what made it funny."

She looked away, still smiling he noticed as she turned. "Guy jokes. I don't think I even want to know."

He moved around to her other shoulder and pushed on the sewed skin and tissue beneath it.

Melanie flinched. "Ow."

"You felt that?"

"Yeah. It hurt my arm. Don't do that again, please."

"That's a good sign then." He dropped the sheet covering her body and let it flow. It waved back and forth beneath her several times then stopped. Without her legs emerging from inside it, the dummy image seemed complete. All she needed was a few pins sticking out of her.

He pushed the thought aside. It wasn't fair to her. She was still his wife, damn it, not some joke.

"Let me go fix you up some sausage, sweetie," he said. "Want the light on or off in here?"

"Can't you take me in the kitchen with you?"

"No," he shot back without realizing how quickly he had snapped at her. He looked at the floor, counted to five, then braved her gaze again. Her eyes wrinkled as though she would cry, even though he knew her tear ducts were drained and dry. But the hurt was honest, regardless, and it had been his fault. "I'm sorry, sweetie. Not yet. I've managed to keep it clean and fairly anti-bacterial in the studio, but if I take you out before I seal up all the wounds you might get infected again," he lied.

"Oh," she said, dropping her gaze. "Okay."

"Soon, I promise. Very soon."

"Sure," she said barely above a whisper. "I trust you."

Mark sat at his desk in the living room, watching the newscasts on his computer monitor. The world was gradually coming back under control, it seemed. Most of the infected dead were safely corralled, although some had been allowed to reintegrate into something that faintly resembled a human existence.

But that would not do for Melanie, not for his Melanie at all. She would not just exist as something less than human. He couldn't let her. Not if he really believed all those things he had promised her during their wedding.

A screensaver slideshow scrolled across the screen. Photos from their wedding. Honeymoon. Melanie pregnant with William and Rebecca. Melanie and her twin sister Melinda dressed as vampires for Halloween. The birth. Lillian in her prenatal chamber until her lungs were strong enough to breathe air well enough. Melanie and the kids at Rock City crammed into the Fat Man's Squeeze. Three gravestones topped with marble crosses.

He tapped the space bar to turn off the slideshow. The news page filled the screen once again.

No. Some limited limbo existence wouldn't do for his wife. Not after all they'd been through together. Not even after all she had done when she crawled out of her grave and returned home. Not even that.

But she hadn't eaten the sausage though. That bothered him. She had tried, then had spit it out onto the floor in a thick mixture of dried blood and partially chewed food and even some of the deteriorated lining of her throat.

"I can't eat that shit," she had yelled. "You've cooked all the flavor out of it."

And he had made more, cooked it less, just enough to make the pink disappear. Too close still to raw for him to dare take a bite.

But it hadn't mattered. She spit that out too and demanded something still more raw.

That's when he had lost it and yelled at her, smashed the plate into the ground and stormed off, stopping only to flip off the lights and slam the door behind him.

He was losing her. He would have to hurry.

It had taken two days of searching the web, but in the end he had the answer. It had been in front of him since the beginning, but he had been too concerned about her humanity to notice something so simple, so beautifully apparent.

Wax.

Sure, she could still feel pain, but not like she had before she had died. And once the brief pain had died down, she would have an alluring new skin, one that couldn't die, one that would remain gorgeous and lustrous, one that would hide the thing she had become underneath.

A visit to a retail supplies website had shown him how to take away the shame of being a mere torso. With the right metal connectors set in place in the flat skin of her shoulder and leg joints, he could purchase new arms, new legs, and limbs for lots of poses and occasions.

Melanie could and would be the lady of the house again, someone elegant and enviable, not a monster to be either pitied or hunted and rounded up or destroyed.

She would be perfect again, just as he wanted her to be. Just as he was sure she herself wanted to be.

After two weeks he was finally finished. He celebrated by hanging up all the mirrors he had taken down when she first returned home and replacing all the light bulbs in the rest of the house that he had taken out. For nearly a month he had been resigned to life in just the studio, living room and kitchen, but now the time had come to welcome Melanie back into the world, the beautiful world she at last belonged to again, thanks to his hard work.

He had even called Melinda, telling her he had a wonderful surprise for her.

"Isn't she amazing?" he asked when he ushered Melinda into the studio.

"What the fuck is that?" Melinda backed into the living room and nearly fell over the ottoman he and Melanie had bought together in the Smoky Mountains at a consignment shop. "Mark, what the hell is that—that thing?"

"It's Melanie. It's my wife." He followed his sister-in-law into the living room and took her hand. "It's your sister."

Melinda snatched her hand away and raised it to slap him. She stopped though, and let her arm drop to her side. "That thing is not my sister. I don't know what you did, but that is not my fucking sister."

Mark walked back into the studio and stood behind his

wife's new body. Long, slender legs that reflected the sunlight in the room emerged from beneath a floral-print sun dress. Matching arms hung by her side, snapped in place on the fixtures that were now a permanent part of her shoulder joints. Even her face was perfect. A combination of make-up and wax gave the illusion that Melanie was as fine a doll of human perfection as had ever existed.

"I didn't have a lot to work with at first," he said. "Most of her was falling off or rotten, but once I decided to use wax and mannequin joints, it all really came together."

"You've turned her into some sort of…" Melinda dropped to her knees. Her voice gave out for a moment. "Some kind of doll or something."

Mark shook his head. "No, Melinda. It's really her." He turned to Melanie. "Tell her, honey. Tell her who you are."

"It can talk?"

Melanie smiled at her sister and nodded. "Yes, I can talk," she said.

"Holy shit."

"My voice isn't what it used to be, but I can still talk."

"You—" Melinda turned from Melanie to face Mark instead. "It, that thing, whatever it is, it's not my sister."

"It's really me, Lin. I'm really Mel. Mark told me all about what happened. About how I died and came back sick, and how he planned to make me better."

"Oh my God."

"I know," Melanie said, coughing, but nothing came up this time. Mark was sure he had cleaned out all the dried blood and mucous. "It's like some kind of miracle."

Melinda pressed against the ottoman and stood up. She marched over to Mark and slapped him hard.

"You bastard. You fucking bastard."

Then she turned and stormed out of the studio, out of the living room, through the front door and all but ran to her Tahoe.

"I'll be right back, Mel. I'm sorry," Mark said and took off after her.

"Melinda!" he shouted from the porch.

"This… This is… You're crazy." She stood in front of her car.

Even from his position on the porch at least twenty feet away, he could tell that she was shaking. "You don't un—"

"Good God, Mark. I don't understand? You're damn right I don't understand." She stepped back toward the porch slowly, deliberately, heavily. "Who could understand what would possess you to even begin to do this?"

Mark walked to the bottom of the wooden steps. "It's okay. She's fine. The only thing she has in common with those monsters in the corrals is that she prefers to eat raw meat. But as long as she's fed, she's able to focus on the part of her that's Melanie. She lost some of her memories and personality due to deterioration of her brain, but most of her is still in there."

Melinda ground her fingers into fists at her side. "How can you talk about this so clinically? Like you're some kind of goddamn scientist or something." She took a deep breath, deep enough for him to see clearly. "You're an artist, Mark, just a fucking artist, not a biologist or forensic pathologist."

"I know." He stepped off the wood into the grass. "You don't know how wonderful it's been having her back. I was so lonely. So damn lonely after she died."

"Mark."

As she spoke, Melinda continued to approach the house. When she got close enough Mark threw his arms around her shoulders and hugged her and began to cry.

"Don't shut her out. Not now. She's so close to being right again."

Mark heard Melinda sniffle and felt her face rest into her chest.

"Did you really tell her all about what happened? All the stuff she did, even the stuff about the kids?"

Mark didn't answer.

Melinda tried to push away, but he held her tight.

"Damn it, Mark." She relaxed and he pulled her closer. "Did you tell her about the kids? Did you tell her that the night she clawed her way out of her grave she damn near killed you after she ate her three children in their own goddamn bedrooms?"

He shook his head against her. "I couldn't. Not yet."

She let her arms fall to her side again.

"You're a coward."

"I…" he started, but his voice failed.

"No," she said. "No excuses. I *don't* understand, but I know this isn't right."

"I…" he tried again and failed.

"But don't worry. I'm going to help you make this right."

He broke off the hug and looked at her eyes, hard-set and angry. She took his hand. "I'm going to help you destroy that thing. And I'm going to help you move on. I'm going to get you some help, Mark."

She grabbed his hand and pulled him toward the porch. He followed numbly. Nothing was going as he had planned. She was supposed to be happy about having her sister back, happy about him giving her a gift that defied everything the news was saying.

Melinda pulled him into the living room and around the furniture, then finally brought him to back to the studio to stand in front of Melanie again. But instead of letting go of him, she only gripped his hand tighter. He could feel her nails biting into the soft skin between his fingers, her pulse throbbing in her fingertips.

"This," Melinda started, cautiously pointing at Melanie. "This may look like my sister and be made up of what used to be my sister, but this thing is not my sister." She pushed forward and poked the hard wax coating hiding Melanie's real chest.

"Melinda…" Melanie said softly.

"No. This thing may even think it's Melanie and may have some of my sister's memories, but my sister is dead, Mark." She pulled her finger away and poked it into Mark's chest. "Your wife is dead. Melanie died from a brain tumor, and this… creature came back with her parts, at least what you didn't create yourself out of stuff you bought."

"You don't understand, Melinda. It's her brain, her memories. It's her."

Melinda pulled him closer, pressed his head against Melanie's chest. "Do you hear her heartbeat? Does her blood run out if I cut her?" She let him go and he stared at the floor. "You say it has her memories and it has her brain, but what about her soul, Mark? Can you honestly believe this monster could even have a soul? What kind of creature with a soul could eat her own goddamn kids, Mark?" She finally let go of his hand. "My sister could never do that. Your wife could never do that."

"But…" Mark tried to respond but there were no words that would mean anything. He looked into Melanie's eyes, hoping they would give him something to say. They looked tired and weak and old, like she was trying to cry, trying to make her dusty tear ducts prove she was still somehow human.

"This isn't my sister, Mark. This is just another one of your goddamn art projects." Melinda pushed Melanie's chest and her stand wobbled and threatened to fall over twice before settling down flat and still again. As it did, the plastic arms and legs flopped in tandem, continuing a few seconds after the base had stopped. "You want to know how I know this doll-monster isn't my sister, Mark? That's how I know. That's how I fucking know."

Mark looked at Melanie. "Give her time, sweetie. She'll come around. Just let her get to know you again."

"Mark?" Melanie asked in a whisper.

"Yeah?"

"I don't remember."

"It's okay, sweetheart. You don't have to."

"I want to know. I have to know."

Mark nodded.

"Oh my god," Melanie said.

"Shit," Melinda said, then turned and left the room.

"You should have told me," Melanie said. "You should have fucking told me. You should have told me! YOU SHOULD HAVE FUCKING TOLD ME, MARK!"

Mark knew better than to argue with her when she was angry and the dead part of her mind was in control, so he quietly followed Melinda from the room and flipped off the light, leaving his wife to scream obscenities at him.

"It's not like that at all, Melinda," he said, trying to catch up to his sister-in-law. "I mean, it looks like that, I'm not so stupid not to see that, but I didn't do it for art. I did it for her."

Melinda stopped and spun around to face him, her eyes full of fire. "Like hell you did. You did it for you."

He opened his mouth to speak but his throat felt empty and dry.

"Don't even try to deny it." She sat down on the fireplace. "There's only one way to make this right."

He shook his head.

"It's the only way."

"I can't. Not after I just got her back."

Melinda sighed loudly, her breath almost hiss-like in the warm air. "Look at me, Mark."

He didn't look up.

"I mean it. Look at me."

He did as she said.

"I miss her too, but I know that she's gone."

"None of your psychological grieving bullshit, please."

"It's not bullshit, Mark. You have to let her go. This isn't healthy." She stood up. "That thing in there, it's just your attempt to fool yourself into thinking she's still here. You're an artist, and sometimes it's hard for you to know the difference between the symbol of the thing and the thing itself." She walked toward him. "That doll you've made is just the symbol." She sat down on the couch and pulled him down beside her. "It's not the thing itself. It's not *her*."

He leaned into her and rested his head on her shoulder and she pulled him closer. "I can't do it. I can't live without her."

"You have to."

"I can't."

Neither said a word for several minutes, and he let her rock him back and forth, wetting her blouse with his tears and snot. When his strength completely faded, she let him slide his head into her lap and she stroked his face while he spasmed and continued to cry.

"Mark?" she said finally.

He looked up at her, his eyes burning.

"If you can't do it, then I'll do it for you."

He shook his head against her lap.

"It's the only way." She brushed his hair from his face. "I'll help you through this, Mark."

She lifted him so that he was sitting next to her, then she tilted his face close to her own. "We're twins, Mark. I'm more Melanie than that project you created." She lifted his hand and pressed it against her cheek. "Feel that? That's warm. That's real. Not wax. Not plastic."

He tried to pull his hand away but she held it firmly against her face.

"Melinda…"

She shook her head. "Not until you realize the difference."

"I missed her so bad." He leaned forward until his forehead touched hers.

"I do too." She raised her hand to stroke his cheek, then let it rest against his skin.

He closed his eyes. The tears burned behind his lids.

Her thumb brushed his lips.

"Mark."

"I miss her so much."

"I know." Something soft and moist pressed against his lips. "Mark," the something said, moving his own lips before backing away. He felt the empty air suddenly, and felt lonelier than before. "I'll take care of that thing and then take you to get some help. We'll get through this together, okay?"

"I don't think I can do it."

She pushed his head away gently and he opened his eyes.

"Where do you keep the guns?"

He shook his head. "Melanie was afraid of them. Haven't owned one since we got engaged."

"Damn. What about an axe?"

He glanced toward the door. "In the shed. On the wall." He took a deep breath. "She's really not what you —"

Melinda pushed her finger against his lips. "She's really not what you think she is either." She smiled, a wide, genuine smile that almost split her face in two living parts. "Do you want my help or not?"

He sniffed and coughed.

"Just go upstairs and go to sleep. I'll take care of everything down here."

She lifted him to his feet, then opened her purse and gave him two Ambien and got him a glass of water. He took the pills then went upstairs, turning back only once to see her waving him on before she went outside for the axe.

He awoke to the sound of movement downstairs. He sat up in bed and checked the clock. Seven-thirty PM. He'd been out for a few hours. His first thought was to run downstairs and visit Melanie, then he remembered that she most likely would no longer be there.

Melinda had no doubt seen to that.

Even if she had been right, he still wasn't ready to see the bloody spot in his studio where Melanie had been cradled in her stand, slowly becoming again the best representation he could create of the woman he loved.

Maybe he had been thinking only of himself. Maybe he had created a doll to love in place of the real Melanie. Maybe memories and leftover bits of brain matter weren't enough to salvage something as esoteric as a human soul.

Maybe one of Melinda's therapist friends could help him. Maybe he had lost focus or even his sanity somewhere during his project.

But he had seen the glimpses of the real Melanie from time to time. He had read the regret in her dry eyes when she learned what she had done to their kids. That couldn't be faked, not by a living human with full faculties and certainly not by a dead one missing almost a quarter of her brain matter.

He walked to the door and called out to Melinda, "I'm going to grab a quick shower first before I come down. Can you put some coffee on?" He tried to make his voice sound calm, and he hoped she bought the lie. "I'll be down in a minute."

There was no answer, but a pan clinked from inside the kitchen, and he walked past the bed toward the master bath, passing a framed photo of Melanie and him sitting on the back of her dad's boat. Melanie's tiny purple bikini had irritated her dad, but Mark had certainly enjoyed peeling her out of it later that night in the guest bedroom. He took the photo off the wall and shoved it into his sock drawer then closed the drawer.

That part of his life was over now, and like it or not, he would have to move on.

A few minutes later, he emerged from the shower, unshaven, and slipped on a pair of boxers, jeans, a brown tee, and a pair of worn-out flip flops then headed downstairs to begin day one of his new life—without Melanie.

"Melinda?" he called. "I don't smell any coffee. I guess you didn't hear me."

More clatter, but this time from the studio.

"Melinda?"

No answer.

"Mel... Melanie?"

Still no response. Just more noises from the studio.

He walked down the steps, not saying anything, just listening to the sounds from the studio. He took the last step, the one onto the hardwood floor tip-toed to avoid making noise himself. Then around the fireplace and couch, then between the chair and ottoman until barely a foot separated him from the closed studio doors.

"Melinda?" he said as he tapped on the doors.

A huge crash made him jump back.

"Melanie? Is that you, sweetheart?"

Something heavy hit the doors, shaking them on their hinges.

He stepped back a few more steps.

The doors shook again.

"Melanie? Is Melinda in there? Is she okay?"

The doors rattled but stayed closed, and a wordless shriek echoed through the house.

"Melanie," he whispered. "Oh my god, Melanie, what did you do?"

One last hit and the doors swung open.

Melanie lay on the floor, half in and half out of the doorway, her hard wax shell broken and torn mostly away along with her dress. Her fake limbs lay strewn about the floor, and what remained of her body was clothed in a smattering of blood and bits of raw flesh and internal organs. She looked up at him like a bloated, road-kill stump of a snake.

She shrieked at him, locking her rage-hued gaze onto his eyes.

"My god!"

Mark looked past her and saw Melinda, or what was left of her, draped over the stand that had been Melanie's cage as much as it had been her support. Her legs were little more than bone below the knees and several inches from her hips and waist had been gnawed clean away. A pool of black and red ooze puddled around the base of the stand.

"Melanie, why?"

The bloody Melanie thing looked at him again and shrieked. "Fix her too," it said.

"What?"

"Fix her too."

"She came in to kill you."

"Fix her."

"How…"

The Melanie thing shrieked again.

"But…"

"Fucking fix her!"

"You killed her. You ate her legs. She was your fucking sister, and you ate her."

The thing looked at him with eyes of regret. "Fix her. Just fix her like me damn it."

Mark stood frozen in place. "Why? She was your sister."

The Melanie thing stopped moving and rolled onto its back. "She let me out of the stand and laid me on the floor. Then she came at me with the axe and I did the only thing I could to protect myself." It coughed up fresh blood, which drooled from the side of its mouth into the floor. "So I bit her. I was so angry and so hungry at the same time." It wobbled, trying to move onto its side. "I know it was wrong, but you can fix her, just like you fixed me." It looked at his eyes with its own eyes wide. "I know you can."

He looked at the thing with Melanie's face and took a step toward it. Then another and another until he stood over it, its mouth thick with meat and blood just inches from his feet. He squatted before it.

"No."

"Mark?"

"No."

"You have to."

He dropped to his knees then caressed the thing's matted hair. "No."

"Please," it said. "You have to fix her and make her perfect again, like you did for me."

"That was a mistake," he said.

The thing spat blood at him and it landed in a splotch on his jeans. "You bastard. You have to."

"I have to fix everything. That's what I have to do."

"You have to make it all right again."

He stopped stroking its hair and stood up, then stepped over the thing and entered the studio. A few steps more and he stood behind the newly dead thing that had been Melanie's sister. That made two women who had loved him now dead, and one of them was his fault. There was no way around that, no way to make it right. He lifted Melinda's head. Her face was still beautiful if not for the eyes clenched in pain and the grimace her mouth had twisted into.

He checked for a pulse. There was none, not that it mattered. One bite and she'd die of infection anyway. Then the infection would spread and her legless corpse would become a living dead thing just like her sister.

He turned to see the Melanie thing shuffling along the floor toward him.

"You're right. I'll fix everything."

It continued toward him. He lifted Melinda's body and secured it in the frame.

"Thank you," the Melanie thing said. "I'm so sorry. I didn't want to kill her. It just happened."

"Ssshh," he said. "I'll fix it so it won't happen again."

"You're the best, Mark. I love you."

He nodded, then lifted the thing from the floor and laid it on its back on an art supply table. "Stay there. Don't move, or you'll roll off."

He walked outside to the shed and came back with another stand, this one just a plain mannequin stand without the brace for a doll's waist. He placed it on the floor beside the one Melinda was strapped into then strode to the table for the Melanie thing.

"I'm sorry, but I don't have another regular stand." He lifted the putrid torso from the table and held it close to his chest. Blood and bile soaked into his shirt and sopped wet against his hairy chest. "But this will only hurt for a moment, then you'll get used to the sensation."

"Wha—" she started, but shrieked instead when he impaled her body on the pole. As she shrieked, she bit down on his shoulder and tore away several inches of flesh and muscle.

Mark howled in pain and fought to hold onto consciousness. *Weird*, he thought. He could almost *feel* the infection setting in, like a tingling dance through his arteries and veins, looking for the quickest path to either his heart or brain.

He'd have to hurry.

"Mark?" it said.

"Ssshh," he answered. "It's okay."

He pulled his torn shoulder away and left her stuck there, impaled on the stand beside her sister. As he turned to leave, he could have sworn he saw Melinda's left leg begin to twitch.

It wouldn't be long now.

"I'll be right back," he said.

He left the studio doors wide open and returned to the shed. Tearing off the old U-Haul sheets, he uncovered the cast-iron safe that had belonged to his grandfather. The old man had kept all the money and receipts from his general store in it, but Mark had put it to a different use.

He spun the combination and swung open the door, revealing a shotgun, two pistols, and a .22 rifle.

He had not really lied to Melanie about getting rid of them. He had just not meant that he had thrown them away. Besides, he hadn't so much as touched one of the goddamn things since the engagement.

He glanced around the shed for another option. The gas can.

He picked it up and tossed it across the shed. Empty. No good at all.

The guns were the only option.

He loaded the shotgun, a 12-guage he had used to hunt deer way back in what seemed now like another life altogether, and shoved a handful of shells into his front pocket.

As he stood up, he caught his reflection in a small mirror that hung on a coiled wire from the ceiling. The shoulder was a mangled mess, but luckily the thing had bitten his right shoulder. Apparently, he'd finally discovered the advantage to being left-handed.

It burned like hell though.

Hurry, he thought. *Just fucking hurry the hell up.*

"Melanie," he yelled as he entered the house. "It's going to be all right."

He stood in the doorway, raised the shotgun, and didn't wait for the monster to figure out what he was doing.

Blam!

A massive hole ripped through Melinda's forehead and splattered the mulch of her brains all over the wall behind her.

"Mark?"

"I fixed her, okay." He opened the chamber and took out the used shell then loaded another. "And now I'm going to fix you too."

The thing twisted and contorted on its stand, shrieking at him, and shook violently until the heavy, flat base actually started to topple.

Mark closed his right eye. Squeezed.

Blam!

The stand and the thing impaled on it stopped moving.

"I'm sorry," he said then turned and left the studio.

His head had begun to feel like blades twisting in both temples, and he sat down to take out the empty shell. He looked at it, twirling it in his fingers twice before setting it down on the coffee table. Then he shoved another shell inside and stuck the barrel in his mouth.

He closed his eyes, both of them.

Finger resting on the trigger.

Squeezing just enough to feel the tension.

The doorbell rang and there was a series of frantic knocks on the door.

"Mark," said an old man's voice, "Are you okay? We heard a shot."

He put the shotgun down on the cushion beside him.

"I'm in here," he said, recognizing the voice. "I'll get the door."

"What was that shot?" An old woman's voice this time.

"Just scaring off some rabbits," he said. "Hang on. I'll unlock the door."

He stood up and walked to the door. His shoulder had stopped burning. He looked at his hands. They were a little pale.

"Melinda said she was coming up to see your new project. She thought it would be fun if we surprised you and came up too." The old woman's voice kept chattering on through the door. "But we got held up with Davey wanting to stop at the all-you-can-eat seafood place. You know how he gets and how long that can take."

"I…" Mark sniffed the air, noticing his hunger growing. "I understand."

He unlocked the deadbolt and opened the door.

THE END

About the author: Sean Taylor is an award-winning writer of stories. He grew up telling lies, and he got pretty good at it, so now he writes them into full-blown adventures for comic books, graphic novels, magazines, book anthologies and novels. He makes stuff up for money, and he writes it down for fun. He's a lucky fellow that way.

He's best known for his work on the best-selling Gene Simmons Dominatrix comic book series from IDW Publishing and Simmons Comics Group. He has also written comics for TV properties such as the top-rated Oxygen Network series The Bad Girls Club. His other forays into fiction include such realms as steampunk, pulp, young adult, fantasy, super heroes, sci-fi, and even samurai frogs on horseback (seriously, don't laugh). However, his favorite contribution to the world will be as the writer/editor who invented the genre and coined the term "Hookerpunk."

Concerning Mister Suffolk

Teel James Glenn

Prologue:

Night Work

Braxton chose a rainy moonless night to bury her near the lawn jockey statue. It had to be a moonless night because the statue beside the bench was visible from the road and half a dozen of the nearby houses, but then, that is exactly why he chose it as a spot to inter the woman he had murdered.

He moved the bench aside and dug directly beneath it as fast as he could, so as not to tempt fate and attract attention by his presence. The earth was softer beneath as well since no one had packed it in.

In less than a half hour the hole was deep enough for the petite form encased in his old canvass sea bag. It made no bulge when he repacked the dirt atop it and carefully replaced the grass.

In the days to come he would come out to sit on the bench under the watchful eye of the statute, wave at the neighbors and gloat in his cleverness.

To know, *know* that the nagging bitch of a wife was gone by his hand, dispatched to the hell she was trying to drive him to with her incessant whining.

Braxton could still feel the sensation of her skull cracking beneath the swinging metal fireplace poker and he squeezed the shovel in his hand hard. The rain dripped off his brow and stung his eyes but he could not blink.

He stared at the three-foot statue of the lawn jockey, resting on its pedestal, so that when he stood beside it he was almost eye-to-eye with the painted cast-iron figure.

The expressionless face of the metal figure seemed alive with movement as the cascading water slid off his painted features. The black lined eyes of the jockey were pointed off, away from the mansion, and it gave Braxton the impression that the statue was purposely looking away from him as if it were judging him.

Braxton could hear Charlene's voice in his head again "I swear, since you came back I get more conversation from Mister Suffolk than you," she would say referring to the pet name she had given the statue in the years gone by, "and at least he doesn't interrupt me when I talk to him."

And talk she did; every day she would take a book to sit on the bench and read and gaze out across the New Hampshire hills. She would look up at the metal figure and talk her heart out.

Braxton would watch her from the upper windows of the house and in profile could see her lips moving. Sometimes she would cry, sometimes laugh but always she spoke her inner feelings to her unmoving suitor. Braxton came to hate the statue as he came to hate her sneering tolerance of him.

Charlene never knew he took up the spyglass and watched her. She never knew he was reading her lips.

It was a skill he had picked up in the days when he had worked the carneys before the war when his name had not been Braxton. That was before he met Charlene and romanced her and married her for her inheritance. It allowed him to climb from the shadows in his new identity as Jonnie Braxton, merchant sailor and respectable husband to the former Charlene Suffolk.

She never suspected that he knew she was going to leave him.

And she never suspected that he knew she told the pagan image that she was going to see that he was discharged from the family shipping line where he was an executive. And worse, she was going to change her will to see that he didn't inherit the house and land. She was going to leave it to Beverly, her niece.

Braxton began to vibrate with rage when he remembered her laughing face when he confronted her about it.

"Of course I want this farce of a marriage over with once and for all," she said.

He trembled with recalling it and he lashed out with the shovel at the metal simulacrum of a man just as a flash of lightening and a peel of thunder rent the air. The flat spade slammed into the belly of the figure with a hard clack sound.

The echo of the strike lingered after the thunder in the night air.

Braxton cursed. The jockey figure mocked him with its stoic stare.

"Blast you," he hissed, "You stand and wait till Perdition for her to come and whisper in your ear some more: I'm goin' into my house to enjoy some fine Port and a smoke for a night's work well done."

Mister Suffolk stood and stared and said nothing.

CHAPTER 1

IN THE ROOST

Jonathon Braxton was the image of a wealthy and successful shipping merchant. He was tall and had the robust carriage of former seaman. He was just past forty and sported an out of date handlebar mustache that, like his thinning hair was a dark red.

He dressed to befit his station as an officer of the shipping firm of Suffolk, Collins and Jones out of Portsmouth New Hampshire.

The offices of the shipping company were in a stable and staid three-story building overlooking the Piscataqua River in Portsmouth Harbor.

"Good morning, sir," Jill, his secretary said as he stepped out of the elevator cage on his floor. "Wet night last night."

"Yes it was," he said with a sly smile, "but April showers bring May flowers." He made a mental note to pay a little more attention to the girl now that he had a 'freer' hand.

"Well you are in a good mood," she said, "and you'll need it; Mister Harrison wants to see you as soon you are in."

"Even that stuffed shirt can't darken my mood today," he said, "Tell him if he wants to see me he can come in to my office in five minutes."

Braxton went into the walnut paneled office and tossed his coat and hat to the couch. He walked straight to the window and looked out over the harbor to survey his empire.

His empire.

Not his wife's now, but his to do with as he wanted; and he had plans. Big plans.

"But first I have to deal with Harrison," he thought.

"'Morning, Jonathon," Micah Harrison said as he entered the office.

Harrison was a college man who had been a naval officer in the pacific theatre. He was blond and would have had an easy time with the ladies if he had not been so single minded about business. Braxton had seen the way even Charlene looked at the blue-eyed businessman.

Worse still, Harrison had opposed many of Braxton's plans to expand the company, and Charlene had sided with him. Now he would show the high and mighty lieutenant Harrison of the United States Navy who was boss.

"Glad you could come in, Harrison," Braxton said, "I wanted to-"

"What the heck are you doing sending our stores to Portland on the first? We need that-"

"Wait right there-"Braxton said, "We will need those provisions when the Lady Of Bristol docks there."

"She's scheduled to dock here on the second."

"Not anymore," Braxton said, "I wired the captain to put into Portland to pick up that shipment of textiles from Abnerville."

Harrison looked shocked, "We discussed that last week and we weren't going to take that contract."

"You and Charlene decided that," Braxton said, "without consulting me; but she changed her mind when I explained it to her."

"What?" Harrison said, "She would never do that; her father and Abnerville mills were feuding for twenty years."

"Her father is dead," Braxton said pointedly. "And I run things now."

"Let Charlene tell me that," Harrison said, "Then I'll believe it."

"I am your boss,' Braxton said, "and I am telling you that we do business with Abnerville now."

The blond glared at the older man with shock in his eyes and anger boiling in the depths. "I will not take your word for that. I want to speak to Charlene - get her on the phone."

Braxton turned and stepped straight to the younger man so that he stood almost nose-to-nose with Harrison.

"You do not tell me what to do, Harrison; I tell you. And if you want talk to my wife you'll have to do it long distance," Braxton said, "She's gone to visit friends in Canada out West."

"I will not order that-"

"I just told you what you will do."

"I don't believe that Charlene would leave on a trip and not stop in the office," Harrison said.

"Oh, you don't?" Braxton said, "I suppose you know my legal spouse better than I do?"

This brought Harrison up short and he looked confused. "But she was so set on us not dealing with-"

"I have this with me," Braxton said producing a folded sheet of paper and thrust it at his underling. "Read it if you doubt she would leave without consulting you."

Harrison read the note with wide eyes and trembling lips. *"Dearest Jonathon,"* it began, *"I know we have been at loggerheads of late, but I do think you have the head for business I do not; I realize that now when I consider that silly feud my father had with Abnerville. I think I need to get away for a bit and clear my thinking. Then, perhaps we can begin anew when I return. I will let you know where I end up;*

Your loving, wandering wife,

Charlene."

Harrison stood staring at the missive open mouthed and slack jawed. Then he looked up at Braxton who stood with a smile on his lips.

"I-uh-"Harrison began, "I find this so hard to believe."

"Well believe it," Braxton said. "My wife is lot smarter than both of us; she knew when to step away and take that deep breath and let me work." He walked to the door and opened it. "Now get out and put that order in."

When Braxton closed the door he held up the letter and kissed it.

"My best work yet," he said. "I'm a regular Rembrandt."

Another of the skills he had mastered in his carny days was forgery. He had been practicing Charlene's signature for months, forging her name to some order bills, small things she would never notice, to put extra money into his pocket. Little did he realize how it would serve him in providing a perfect alibi for her disappearance.

A simple note to start it, to explain her sudden exit from his life and then a series of letters, each more despondent until a final note when she threatened suicide.

"Perfect," he laughed, "No proof she's dead for seven years that way—more than enough time for me to loot every penny from this company."

The rest of the day went well; the word that Charlene was gone on a holiday was all through the building by lunchtime. He saw the looks of pity from many of the women and a little bit of fear from most of the men.

He liked it; the power that fear of him gave him. If he could not have their respect he would take their fear. He could build a powerbase on fear.

"See you tomorrow, Jill," he said cheerfully as he headed out the door at closing, "don't stay too long."

He drove home with a pleasant image of Jill in his bed and then went through the list of available women at the company; women that had been off limits while he had Charlene's scrutiny to worry about. He'd had to keep his mistress in Nashua to be safe. Now the sky was the limit.

As he drove up the main road to the mansion he saw the lawn jockey and the bench on the gentle rise that gave a view of the entrance. Both were silhouetted by the setting sun and try as he might he could see no telltale sign of the grave beneath the seat.

The figure of the metal sentry seemed to be facing slightly

off from what he remembered and then he recalled that he had struck it the night before.

"Good thing I didn't knock it off the base altogether," He thought, "It would only have drawn attention to it."

He drove on past it and then watched it in the rearview mirror and because of the change in its orientation he had the odd feeling that it was watching him.

"I've got to get rid of that damn thing as soon as it seems safe to make changes like that."

He ate a dinner of leftovers in the large wood paneled dining room of the house, feeling the emptiness of the place.

Braxton left the dishes on the table and sat in his study after dinner looking out the windows toward the lawn. There was a faint glow of Portsmouth beyond the dark shape of the statue. The unmoving figure was like a mote in Braxton's eye.

Rather than feel satisfaction at seeing the bench beneath which his jailer-wife now rested, he felt anger for seeing the scarecrow figure. He had the unreasoning desire to race out with an axe to smash the stoic face to scrap.

"Get ahold of yourself, Jonnie boy,' He thought, "it's all in hand—all taken care of. Just ride the storm all out." He lit a cigar - something Charlene had not permitted in the house - and tried to relax.

Now he could speed up his looting the company, hide his assets and be gone in four or five years with all the money he would ever need.

"And I'll melt you to a pile of slag long before that, you metal bastard," he murmured to the distant jockey. "Maybe I'll recast you as a spittoon and drop you in my favorite brothel in Boston." The thought made the ex-mariner laugh long and loud. He finished his cigar and went off to bed with a backward glance toward the jockey.

That night the storm rolled in again from the North Atlantic booming loud and slashing the night with white hot lightening. The sky show yanked the murderer from his slumber with explosive abruptness.

He shot bolt upright and in the fading glare of the lightening he saw a figure standing in the corner of the room.

"Who is that?" Braxton grabbed for his pistol beneath his pillow and thrust it at the dark shape. "Speak up!"

But there was no sound or movement from the shadows.

"Speak up or I'll shoot!" he rose from the bed keeping the pistol pointed at the spot where he had glimpsed the figure. "I mean it!"

Still there was no sound but the pelting rain on the windows. He raised the gun to fire it at the moment another peel of thunder rattled the house and a slash of lightening lit the room.

Braxton gasped; the figure of the Mister Suffolk was standing in the angle of the room!

Braxton fired the gun until the hammer clicked on empty. Still he pulled the trigger until another lightning bolt flashed light into the room to show there was nothing in the corner.

The murderer ran to the light switched and clicked the light on.

There were six bullet holes in the wall of the room, nothing else.

Braxton stood with his arm extended, his muscles locked and shaking for minutes as blast after blast of thunder rocked the house. In each flash of light the stark shadows of the window frame crawled across the room to mark the space where the phantom had been.

Braxton threw his gun down and raced to the window. In the flashes he saw the figure of the Jockey and the black slashes of the bench.

"You bastard!" he screamed the top of his voice.

Then he realized what he had done and began to laugh hysterically, laugh until his shoulders jerked violently. He slumped against the sill on his knees, his cheek against the cold glass feeling the vibrations of the storm outside. He stayed there until the storm had passed and the rain had stopped.

When he pulled himself to his feet he looked out again

at the figure on the lawn.

"Yeah, bastard," he said aloud, "A spittoon."

Chapter II

Bowled over

The next day at work Jill's greeting was subdued. "Why, Mister Braxton," she said, "You look-"

"I didn't sleep well, Jill," he said following the axiom that the lie should be close to the truth make it work, "I was worried about Mrs. Braxton."

"Of course, sir," the girl said. "Mister Harrison left this message for you." She held up an envelope and he took it from her and opened it.

"*I hereby render my resignation effective immediately,*" Braxton read aloud. Jill gasped.

"Oh my!" she said.

Braxton worked hard not keep from giggling before he got into his office and closed the door. Then he went to his bottom drawer and had a celebration drink.

He sat back and put his feet up on the desk and sipped his drink slowly. "Better and better," he said aloud.

"Mister Braxton," Jill's voice over the intercom broke him from his reverie, "Miss Suffolk is here."

He sat upright. "Excuse, me?" he asked.

"Miss Beverly Suffolk." Jill said. "Shall I send her in?"

"Yes," Braxton said, "Go ahead."

He was on his feet when the pretty brunette twenty year old came through the door.

'Beverly," he said in a cheerful voice, "So wonderful to see you."

"Jon," she said with a subdued voice, "I heard that Aunt Char is gone; what's it all about?" Then she lowered her eyes, "Did you two have a fight?"

Braxton had been expecting a visit from the girl, but not so soon. He put on his best chagrined manner.

"Beverly," he said in a voice barely a whisper, "I was going to call you today—Here." He held out the forged note from his dead wife, wrinkled and smudged as if he had been pouring over it. Braxton knew that to work a con the little details had to be worked out.

She read the note with knit brows and a pouting mouth. When she looked up her face was fixed in a questioning expression. "I –uh I knew you two had been having some-uh difficulties, Jon," she said, "But I know Aunt Char wanted to make it right. I just don't-"

"Beverly," Braxton said. "Maybe we can talk about it later; come over for dinner? The house seems suddenly very empty without her."

He could play the deserted, injured party to the hilt and all the simpleminded yokels in Portsmouth would fall for it.

Should be good for quite bit of sympathy and attention; maybe even soft shoulder from little Beverly here, he thought to himself.

"Of course, Jon" she said rising, "I'll come by—say seven?"

"Yes," he said rising to meet her at the door, "Seven would be fine." He leaned in to kiss her on the cheek and accept a hug of condolence from her.

"You take care, Jon," she said with real concern, "You don't look well."

"I'll be alright," he said, "Work will be the best medicine."

After he closed the door he had a hard time wiping the smile from his face. He thought of the seduction scene in Richard III and had a giggle that he might be able to bring the scenario to life with Beverly.

"I have to have a dinner for her, however," he thought, "and have my mess cleaned up." He called Jill and had her find him an agency to engage a woman to clean the house, and a cook. He then dove into his work so that he could leave at lunchtime and go to the mansion before the cleaning woman could arrive to pack some of Charlene's things in a suitcase to make it look like she left of her own free will. He stood on the porch with the suitcase that contained his 'proof' that Charlene had left, and looked out on the lawn. The figure of the jockey and the hidden grave were brightly lit by the noontime sun as if illuminated by spotlight.

Braxton put the suitcase in the trunk of his sedan with plans to drop it into the sea at the first chance he got to complete the illusion of Charlene's trip. He went back to work and enjoyed the remainder of the minutia of the business day while fanaticizing about his pleasant dinner to come with Beverly.

He drove home with a light spirit and even waved to Mister Suffolk as he drove up the driveway past the metal sentinel. The housekeeper was still cleaning the downstairs, as instructed and the cook, a large Hungarian woman, was busy in the kitchen with the roast beef and potatoes meal she was preparing.

"When will the meal be ready, Mrs. Bodi?" he asked and he took a whiff of the contents of the stove.

"By about seven thirty or so," she said. She was making a cake as she spoke and did not look up. "And that will be lucky; I did not get the call until late this afternoon."

"I'm sure that will be fine," he said with a smile; "I apologize for the late call but, uh, my wife had to leave unexpectedly."

"Don't matter to me," she said, "I do my best."

"I'm sure you will, Mrs. Bodi. I'm going to take shower and get ready for my guest."

Beverly arrived only fifteen minutes late and parked out front next to Braxton's sedan.

"Hi Bev," He said stepping down from the porch.

"Hi Jonathon," she said, "I'm sorry if I'm late; I hope it

won't ruin the dinner."

"Not to worry," he said, "I hired a cook and she says it will be a while." He waved a hand out toward the bench. "Why don't we sit out here and enjoy the sunset while we wait for her to call us."

"That's great idea; Aunt Char's thinking spot."

They went to the bench to sit and talk. Before they did she stepped over to the lawn ornament and touched a hand to the cap on its head.

"Funny little man," she said, "Aunty Char used to talk about how she would come out here and speak to him all the time when she was little girl; when her daddy was at sea; that's how she came to call him 'Mister Suffolk'- she had heard them call her daddy that. So she pretended she was talking to her daddy."

Braxton sat back on the bench taking in the sight of the young girl reminiscing. He watched the play of the failing sun on her cheekbones and the gentle curve of her neck. And most of all the sensual curves of her hips.

"A horse, a horse," he said, "my kingdom for a horse."

"What?" she said turning to look at him.

"Oh nothing, Bev, "he smiled. "Just quoting from a Shakespeare play."

"You weren't listening to me at all!" she chided as she sat down beside him.

"Oh I was, dear," he said, "You were talking about dear Charlene coming down here to talk to Mister Suffolk about all sorts of things. She explained she would talk to this-this 'little fellow' as if he were her oldest and dearest friend."

"In a way he was," the girl said, "She was a lonely girl, she told me. Sort of the poor little rich girl; then when her mother died she took care of her father and sort of stayed to herself. A wallflower."

"I know," He said enjoying with immense delight having this conversation over the corpse of his murdered spouse. "When she went to Boston for meetings with Sloan and Sons

I was working in their receiving office; I knew right away she was special."

Yeah, an easy mark for a smooth talker.

"She was so happy when you two came back together," Beverly said, "You really made her feel wanted."

Her money anyway, the frigid bitch!

"She was a very special woman," he faked, "I hope she can find herself with this—this trip of hers." He accepted a warm hand from the girl and captured it between both of his. "But I can't deny that we were happy at first, but she became... troubled."

"How so?"

"She became distant, self-absorbed," he said working to embellish the lie. "She seemed to come out here every night and spent more time talking to him that to me. It still feels like she's here." He had trouble keeping a straight face when he said that.

He had no trouble keeping the sympathetic eyes of the girl locked with his and knew he was going to get just where he wanted to with her; if not that night, then with patient work, all the way to home base before he cut and ran from Portsmouth.

There was a long quiet moment where their eyes met and then she blushed and turned way toward the jockey. She pulled her hand way and stood up.

"Aunty Char said her daddy told her that this statue had been here as long as anyone could remember," she said in a strained whisper, trying to regain her composure. "She said they always thought of it as the guardian of the family since Grandfather Lucifer Suffolk brought it here from Haiti."

She stepped up to the metal figure and idly ran her hand along the leg of it. "Funny, it seems to be moved a bit, Jon; do you suppose the wind the other night moved it?"

He thought of the shovel strike to the jockey and grinned. "I suppose it was pretty strong." She ran her hands along the base of the statue and then her hand stopped and she leaned in.

"Hey did you know there was writing on this thing?" She

squinted to be able to read it. "It's in a funny sort of language. I can't read it in this light."

She popped up and her face was bright with excitement. "I have to get a piece of paper and rub this so I can read it."

"There's stuff in my desk in the study, Bev," he said with a smile. "Go get it."

She headed into the house to get paper to rub the writing off the pedestal leaving him alone with the metal man.

"It always comes back to you and me doesn't it, Mister Suffolk?"

Braxton took his lit cigar and took the glowing tip and pressed it to the face of the statue, drawing it across to make a mustache on the figure like his own. "Now at least we are two of a kind!"

Beverly came running back with an excited giggle. "The cook said dinner is ready when we come in," she said. She raced directly to the jockey and began to rub the paper on the raised letters around the pedestal in sections.

"It looks like it might be Latin or maybe old French," she said, "But I can take it to my old professor at the university to get it translated." She worked her way around the base of the statue.

"Hey, there's a pentagram among all this stuff."

"Probably some sort of mariner's good luck charm," Braxton said. "You said it came from Haiti, right? Probably a manufacturer warranty!"

They both laughed and she moved around to the front of the statue away from the house. "Oh you have no romance in your soul!" She chided him.

"I've got plenty," he answered, "I just haven't had many chances to show it in a business suit." He cautioned himself not to rush his plans.

"Oh those rotten neighborhood kids!" She blurted out.

"What do you mean?"

"Some little creep has been shooting BB's at Mister Suffolk!"

Braxton shot to his feet and ran to the statue. In the dim light he could just make out six neat dents in the front of the jockey that looked to be made by bullets!

Chapter III

Letters from the Dead

Braxton fled to the house with horror. He went straight to his study and poured a stiff drink of Scotch before she came into the house to join him.

"What is the matter, Jon?" Beverly asked. "Are you alright; shall I summon a doctor?"

Those were my bullet holes in that damn statue; it was in my room. I did shoot it. But how? No, No, Jonnie, you have to realize it's just the strain of it all

"Those kids shooting Mister Suffolk," He said in a soft whisper. "It just upset me; it uh, made me think of how much he meant to Charlene and how much she meant to me." His voice caught in his throat and Beverly had to lean.

"Oh Jonathon," she said reaching to hold his arm. "I'm sorry, I should have thought."

"Just punk hooligans," he said more for his own benefit than hers. "That's all those holes mean; somebody else's bullets."

"I'm sure they can be repaired," she said to reassure him, "a little putty and paint; Old Suffolk could use a new coat of paint anyway." She tried to elicit a smile from him.

"Yes," he said, "I can take him down and put him in the basement to repair him so he'll be just as he was before Charlene went way. Yes." *And then melt the bastard hunk of junk to slag!*

"Dinner is ready, sir," the cook spoke.

"Can you eat, Jon?" Beverly asked. "It would do you good."

"Uh, yes," he said taking one more drink. "I suppose I should. I confess I am not good company."

"I'm sure you will feel better once you've had Mrs. Bodi's good cooking."

"Yes," he said, "I'm sure I will."

He did feel better when he sat at the table and began to eat. His mind was still awhirl with what had happened. His conversation was scattered and distracted. He threw aside all plans to move in amorously on the young girl, at least for that night.

Outside seemed to mirror Braxton's feelings, a sheet of rain and booming thunderclouds began to pelt the countryside.

"I am sorry I am so...so..." He began when they had finished dinner and dessert.

"Oh, please Jon," she said as she donned her jacket to leave, "You don't have to make any apologies." She leaned in and kissed him on the cheek warmly. "Aunty Char is so lucky to have you, Jon."

She blushed and turned quickly to leave.

Maybe it isn't a total loss; I can work on her sympathy later. He watched her drive away and found his gaze arrested by the bronze colored figure at the end of the drive.

"You can leave the plates and things, Mrs. Bodi," he said to the cook. "You'd better get home before it gets worse. I can clear it all away; let's break me in gradually to being taken care of properly."

"Thank you, Mister Braxton," She said, "I'll be by round lunch time to sort out what the pantry needs and then get a start on setting up a menu. Just leave the pots and such to soak; I'll do them then."

"Good night, Mrs. Bodi; get home safe."

He watched her drive off as the storm increased in intensity. When her taillights faded away he felt suddenly and completely alone. The house seemed to grow around him and the sound of the wind-driven rain on the windows echoed and reechoed off the wooden panels of every room.

He went back to his study and poured himself another Scotch. He drank it without even tasting it, all the while his eyes fixed on the window and the darkness beyond where he knew that the lawn jockey was standing.

He could see it in his mind's eye looking out at the road. He could imagine the cast iron figure turning to face the house, somehow inexorably moving toward the house coming to get him!

"Stop it!" he screamed out loud, his own voice startling him. "This is insane. The damn thing is just a freaking statue; those bullet hits on the thing were like she said, from some punk kids shooting at it."

"I'll bring it to the basement and I'll get a blow torch and melt it." He paced back and forth while the wind increased in fury outside the windows.

"Get a hold on yourself, Jonnie," he said, "You killed the bitch and that is that. It's a freakin' lawn toy."

He tried to occupy himself by clearing the table. He flicked on each lamp and bulb as he moved through the rooms so that the house was soon ablaze with light. It was his only weapon against the sense of aloneness he suddenly felt.

"I'll just take an early day tomorrow," he said when he finished the last dinner plate. "Go down to Boston and kick back; tell everyone I'm just going to deal with my nerves over Charlene." He giggled like a truant schoolboy. "And it will be true."

Just then the power went out and the house was immediately plunged into darkness as black as a nightmare.

"Damn!" He froze in the kitchen doorway.

Outside the tempo of the storm changed. In the sudden enveloping darkness of the mansion it seemed to roar.

Braxton stumbled along the wall of the kitchen to where the long matches for lighting the pilot light on the stove where and lit one. With that he found candle and lit it.

"Son of a bitch electric company," he cursed out loud. He moved to the fireplace in the parlor and lit the kindling in it. In five minutes he had a roaring fire going. He located a hurricane lantern and ignited it.

Where all had been black before now the shadows danced and moved around the room. What had been a safe secure home moments before was now alive with moving darkness. It might as well have been a Neolithic cave!

Braxton felt his hands shaking as he held the lantern up to cast the light around the room. He closed the door to the kitchen and then pulled the sliding door to the parlor closed so that he was closed in.

But more important to his way of thinking; *IT* was sealed out.

This is insane. It's just a power failure because of the storm. The lights will come on in a few minutes and I'll grab a bottle and go up to my room and drink myself to sleep. No damn devil doll from Haiti, no boogeyman. Nothing. "He looked out toward the window and a flash of lightening slashed the night sky and illuminated… IT.

It was like a challenge.

"Okay, you bastard," he said, "I will destroy you." He grabbed a slicker and then went out into the driving rain. He ran across the soggy lawn to the rise where the statue stood mocking him.

"I'll make sure you join Charlene in Hell, you piece of junk!" Braxton screamed at the top of his lungs. The raindrops were like shotgun pellets driven against his skin, stinging his face and all but blinding him.

He set the lantern down and wrapped his arms around the jockey. He braced his legs and tried to pull the figure off the pedestal.

"Come on!" Braxton yelled. "Give up!" He strained with all his strength worrying the figure off the base with one mighty heave.

At that moment a massive bolt of lightning ripped from the Heavens and drove into the iron figurine in Braxton's arms.

The murderer was blasted off his feet, flying ten feet across the lawn. The jockey slipped from his limp arms and dropped back to the base again almost exactly as it had been before.

CHAPTER IV

TO BECOME…

Braxton woke with the first rays of morning sunlight edging the trees. He was cold and wet and in pain and for long moment he didn't understand why he was laying on the lawn.

The first thing he saw was the Lawn Jockey statue edged with morning light. It had been slightly turned on the base by his violent 'argument' with it the night before and now was partly facing the house.

It appeared to Braxton as if it were looking at him. At first it did not register but there was something not quite right on it, then Braxton noticed that the face of the statue was different. There was a mustache on the previously clean-shaven face.

Braxton tried to focus his eyes but his head ached and vision was blurred. He pushed himself to his feet and staggered toward the house, his arms and legs stiff.

He almost fell into the entrance hall where all the lights were blazing. He stopped, stripping off his still wet slicker and leaned against the wall trying to draw deep breath. His lungs were on fire. It took him a full ten minutes to recover enough strength to stagger into the kitchen to hang over the sink to scoop some water into his face. When he did he felt hair come away into his hand. He stared at them for a long slice of time.

He held the long white hairs up close to his eyes and then pushed off the sink to look into the mirror-like glass cabinet front. What he saw filled him with dread.

His mustache was falling out in clumps, as was his hair, but more disturbing was that both were stark white.

"My God!" he murmured. He ran his hands through his hair and more came loose in his hands. "The lightning!"

He slumped to his knees and hung on the edge of the sink with no strength to stand. When he did his legs were uncooperative and his knees barely functioned. He had no idea how long he hung there but he was vaguely aware of the sun climbing through the morning mist and the shadows changing as if in a dream.

When he could find his feet again he lumbered into the parlor where the embers of the fire glowed pink and he fell to the couch in exhaustion. His mind was a jumbled collage of images: Charlene's look of shock as he brought the poker down on her head, the face of the lawn jockey as he wrestled it from the pedestal and the look from Beverly when he had fled into the house.

Beverly's expression of concern suddenly gave him hope of some help. He had a sudden desire to hear her voice to talk to her, to beg her to help him; perhaps to forgive him.

Get ahold of yourself, Jonnie; don't go confessing and getting yourself the electric chair!

None-the-less he forced himself to stand and make his way to the phone on the table in the foyer. He fumbled with the receiver and then realized his hands were not responding to his commands, just like his legs were sluggish. He dropped the receiver twice before he could get it to his face but then he could not get the fingers of his left hand to separate so he could dial Beverly's number.

"No!" he rasped in frustration. He stared at the phone and began to cry with the helplessness he felt. He cursed and looked out through the window to see the cast iron figure that had become such pinpoint of horror for him.

"I won't let you win!" he declared. He used his uncooperative fingers to jiggle the cradle until the operator came on the line.

"Operator; can I help you?" a female voice asked.

"Yes," he forced out through uncooperative lips and managed to recite a number.

"One moment please."

It was an eternity until the buzzes and clicks of the phone gave way to ringing and then soft voice answered, "Hello?"

"Beverly," he rasped, "Its Jonathon."

"Jonathon," she said with a shocked tone, "You sound terrible; are you alright?"

"No," he said, "I-uh-could you come out?" The words were getting harder and harder to force though an uncooperative throat. "Please?"

"Oh my goodness," she said, "Of course; it will take me a little bit to get out of the office, but-uh-I'll be there as fast as I can."

"Thank you." He said and dropped the phone to the cradle again.

The effort to stand was telling on him and he staggered back into the parlor bumping into a side table and knocking a lamp over. It crashed to the wooden floor with a deafening and jarring sound in the quiet house.

He looked out the bay window to see the late morning sun illuminating the lone figure in the warm light. He stared at it because it looked wrong. The orientation of it had been changed so that it was facing back toward the house.

There was more. He strained his eyes to peer at it and tried to understand why it looked different to him. Then it occurred to him; the silhouette was changed! The shirt was different, not the horizontally striped riding silk, and the boot line was gone on the trousers.

He couldn't understand it.

He realized he was thirsty again and so tried to rise from the couch but found his legs had completely stopped cooperating with him. He cursed again and grabbed the arm of the couch to try and pull himself up to his feet. That was when he looked down at his own feet and gasped.

"Oh God!" he cried. His lower legs and feet were encased in the same style of riding boots that the Lawn Jockey had been wearing.

This can't be happening. This is wrong! Why would somebody dress me in boots?"

The horror of what he saw gave him strength and he compelled himself to a standing position. He tottered like a drunk, continuing to stare down at his booted feet, his mind a confused storm of thought.

It has to be the same kids who shot Mister Suffolk; yeah, that's it; they saw me get struck by the bolt and this is their twisted idea of fun.

He wondered why his legs were so stiff but he could not concentrate on that because he noticed then that his legs were encased in white riding trousers. He reached down to touch the legs and noticed that the sleeve of his shirt was different.

He raised his arm to look at it close up. It was silk.

He was wearing a cream colored silk shirt.

Braxton turned and staggered at the bathroom and threw himself through the doorway. He hung on the edge of the sink and stared into the mirror.

No!

He was wearing cream colored silk riding shirt with horizontal bronze stripes, white pants. But more horrifying than what was on his body was what had happened to his face. His mustache was completely gone, his hair was all but gone and his features were puffy.

No! No, no!

He brought his hand to touch his face but when he did the skin was cold and stiff. "No!"

He tottered down the hall falling from wall to wall into tables, knocking a mirror off the wall and stumbling into a coat rack.

This is that damn thing; I have to destroy it!

His legs would not bend, his feet felt as if they were lead weights. He knew he had to reach Mister Suffolk. He had to.

I'll destroy you, you bastard!

Mister Suffolk stood unblinking but it was not the figure he had seen even a few hours before; gone was the striped shirt, boots and riding pants. The statue now wore a jacket and tie and conventional trousers all molded perfectly to the cast iron form.

Braxton willed himself to walk stiff-legged across the lawn toward the statue. As he approached it with his tottering and uneven gait he could see that the once smooth features of the statue were now sculpted into firm and more human lines; a strong jaw, aquiline nose and well-formed open eyes. There was a full head of brunette hair and a formed mustache of the same color on the molded figurine.

So well sculpted were the features that the painted flesh tones of face seemed as if they were between breaths.

When his hand touched the arm of the jockey Braxton was horrified to see that his own hand was no longer a mobile and usable one. The fingers were fused and no longer his own.

No! This can't be real!

As if to punctuate his thoughts the hand of the lawn jockey suddenly seized Braxton's and began to pull *him* forward.

The murderer pulled back and just before he could no longer resist the pull he forced one last sound out of his transformed throat.

"No!" and then he was silent forever…

Epilogue:

Homecoming

Beverly drove up to the mansion less than a half hour after she got the urgent call from Braxton. His car was still in its spot by the house.

"Jonathon!" she called as she burst through the doorway into the foyer. "I got the rubbing translated; it was Haitian French and said- oh!"

She came up short when she entered the parlor, startled by the figure in the overstuffed chair.

"Oh my," she said, "I was expecting-"

"Oh, I know," the figure said, "Mister Braxton has gone to join his wife; our relative."

"Relative?" She said confused. "I thought that Jonathon was an orphan."

"Oh I mean our relative, Miss Suffolk - Beverly. Suffolk is my last name as well."

She stared in confusion at the dark shape in the chair. The sharp shadows from the bright sunlight kept the features shaded. "You said Jonathon went to Aunty Charlene? Are they going to make up?"

"I don't think so; but they will be together." The strange man stood up and stepped forward into a shaft of light. His features were strong with a square jaw and slightly old-fashioned mustache. His eyes were piercing blue and his smile relaxed.

"What are you doing here?" she asked. She looked at him with curious eyes and could clearly see the lines of her father and aunt's features echoed in the stranger's.

"This was my home once. I've come back." He placed a gentle hand on her arm and walked her unresistingly back out the door and across the lawn to the bench. When they both were standing by the bench he turned to her and added, "You said you had translated something?"

"Yes, "she said, "I did a rubbing off of the statue; it is a funny sort of poem."

"Please," he said, his eyes sparkling with humor. "Tell me what it says."

"*What was dark is light; what was day is night; who was live is lone and who was gone is home.*' See," she added, "Silly." She went to the statue to run her hand along the base.

"Oh, not necessarily," the newcomer said. "Quaint perhaps, but not silly."

She took her hand from the pedestal and touched the cast iron boot of the jockey. "Poor fellow is so—oh,"

"What is it?" the stranger asked. "Is something wrong?"

"He was all pitted with some bullet holes but now he's all good as new; even better. He looks like he's had a fresh coat of paint."

"He?"

"Mister Suffolk-" she said.

"Yes?" the stranger said.

She laughed, "Oh yes, that is your name too, isn't it?"

"Yes," He said, "but it's not the only one I have. You can call me by the other one."

"And that is?" She found herself smiling broadly at the handsome stranger. She hoped he was a very distant cousin.

"It is a name I hope I will hear you say often." He said with a soft, almost musical voice, "My name is Lucifer."

The End

About the Author: Teel James Glenn. Winner of the 2012 Pulp Ark 'Best Author of the Year.' Epic ebook award finalist. P&E winner 'Best Thriller Novel', "Best Steampunk Short",

Multiple finalist "Best Fantasy short stories," Collection"
Author of the bestselling *Exceptionals* Series, The *Maxi/Moxie*
Series, The *Dr. Shadows* Series, The *Renfairies* series and others.
Visit him at www.theurbanswashbuckler.com

OTHER WORKS

BY DREAMING BIG PUBLICATIONS

Esther's eighth birthday.

The day that her mother, Charlotte, had been fearing.
As a teenager, Charlotte had gotten involved in a satanic cult and had made a promise to Satan that he could have her firstborn child. At the time, she really didn't believe any of this was true. It was just a silly thing she did to fit in.
But now…

Can Charlotte save Esther from Satan's grip? Or is she destined to fulfill that long-ago promise?

Other Works

by Dreaming Big Publications

Nelleke Reitsma is one of the world's top lutenists and guitar players. She is very good because she has had 350 years to practice. Sinfonia: First Notes on the Lute records her life, beginning with her entrance into the world of the undying through friendship with Izaak, a mysterious young man who only comes out at night; and, eventually, her crossing over into that world. Leaving her native Netherlands for England, she finds herself embroiled in a fight to save the vampire community of London from destruction. She encounters Shakespeare and Queen Elizabeth, and, using her connections to government and the theater, uncovers the last followers of an ancient religion that possesses power capable of destroying Nelleke and the coven of vampires to which she belongs. It is up to her to stop them. A fascinating and compelling piece of paranormal fiction, it abounds in danger, romance, horror, love, and beauty.